THE SICKNESS CALLED MAN

FERDINANDO CAMON

THE SICKNESS CALLED MAN

TRANSLATED FROM THE ITALIAN BY JOHN SHEPLEY

T M P

THE MARLBORO PRESS / NORTHWESTERN

EVANSTON, ILLINOIS

The Marlboro Press/Northwestern
Evanston, Illinois 60208-4210

Originally published in Italian under the title *La malattia chiamata uomo*. Copyright © 1981 by Garzanti Editore s.p.a. English translation copyright © 1992 by John Shepley. Published 1992 by The Marlboro Press. The Marlboro Press/Northwestern edition published 1996. All rights reserved.

Printed in the United States of America

ISBN 0-8101-6015-3

Library of Congress Cataloging-in-Publication Data

Camon, Ferdinando, 1935–
    [Malattia chiamata uomo. English]
    The sickness called man / Ferdinando Camon : translated
from the Italian by John Shepley.
        p.   cm.
    ISBN 0-8101-6015-3 (paper : alk. paper)
    I. Shepley, John. II. Title.
PQ4863.A392M3513   1996
853'.914—dc20   96-16599
                                                    CIP

The paper used in this publication meets the minimum require-
ments of the American National Standard for Information
Sciences—Permanence of Paper for Printed Library Materials,
ANSI Z39.48-1984.

All things are full of labour;
man cannot utter it.

Ecclesiastes 1 : 8

CONTENTS

THE SICKNESS CALLED MAN

PART ONE

1. He

For seven years we met, four times a week, in his house, we spoke for 1,050 hours, but I don't know exactly who he is. It seems to me he's fairly tall, but I may have this impression because the only moment when I had him in front of me and could look him in the face was when I had rung the bell and he came to open the door: for a moment he was there before me, in broad daylight, standing upright against the shadow of the small, poorly lighted hallway, with his left hand resting on the door handle while he slowly extended his right hand toward me. I reached for that hand and shook it as though by habit, but in reality listening in those two or three seconds, with my fingers, skin, and nerves, to the warmth, strength, and adhesion of his fingers, skin, and nerves. At the same time I hastily scrutinized his face in the hope of receiving from it the greatest possible number of sensations. He smiled with his eyes and mouth, staring at me for a moment in expectation of my greeting, and in that moment an understanding was established between the two of us stronger than any pact; I felt infected and invaded by his assurance, I seemed to be greeting him because that is the custom, but actually it was to make him hear my gratitude in my voice. I slipped in beside him and took those few (twelve, thirteen, fourteen) steps to reach my place. While taking those few steps, I tried to fix his image and keep it from dissolving. I froze his words, listened to them again, extracted their meaning, seeking a fresh answer to the same question: how had I been welcomed? how was he today? what was his tone of voice? had he . . . perhaps . . . smiled? And then I recalled his silhouette, and realized that in looking at him I had looked up from below, he was therefore taller than I, but outside the doorway there were three steps and while waiting I always stood on the middle one: it was his arrival that drew me up and inside.

He wasn't always smoking when he came to the door. Sometimes he started smoking during the session, and then all of a sudden I'd hear the click of his cigarette lighter, repeated several times until the flame caught and stayed lighted. After a moment or two I heard the first puffs. And then immediately came the first clouds of smoke, light, invisible, impalpable, but penetrating. I was breathing what he breathed.

I can't say anything more about him. A thousand hours were not all that many, and the seven years went by with the speed of a satellite passing on the horizon. I aged in those seven years, but without being aware of it. I suffered more than I could bear. At times the suffering was so overwhelming, so inescapable, so rooted within me, that I wondered how I could stand it, and only now do I see why: because I was not only myself, but him as well. I was two.

His house was outside the city, in the hills beyond the outskirts; it took half an hour's drive to get there. His consulting room was in one corner of the house. My place was in one corner of his consulting room. In leaving the city, I separated myself from my history, detached myself from my surroundings, and for half an hour navigated in a space that was neither mine nor his, like an astronaut emerging from the earth's gravity but not yet drawn into a lunar orbit.

Already the sight of the hills where he lived had a liberating effect that is hard to express, but then everything I'm telling is hard to express, and there are certain prerequisites for listening to it if it's to be understood: a familiarity with speech more than with other forms of communication, and an ability to glimpse the endless symbolic relations that unite all things and form a web along which, without our realizing it, they constantly travel and change position. I went to him every week for seven years, but I was never able to say why and always felt that if the day ever came when I'd be able to say it I would stop going. The problem was a linguistic one, and therefore absolute.

And it was not a problem outside myself: I was the problem. There was only one way to confront it: I had to become him and he me.

This identification consisted in the use of the same language: he had to speak like me. Our relationship was a continual search, with him looking for me, me sending out signals, and him letting me know he had received them and coming ever closer. It was like walking in one of those houses of mirrors, where every time you take a step your image comes back to you from all sides, the door is disguised as one of those sides, but you can't tell which, and after half an hour you're lost. Whereupon the unseen owner of the labyrinth, who nevertheless can see you, guides your steps by making you move more to the right, more to the left, ahead, back, until with the last step you find yourself facing the world or facing him, which comes to the same thing.

The most delicate moment of every session was the initial one. The first word was the most difficult. It raised a mountain of meanings, which moved in all directions, as when a surfacing whale feels thousands of little fishes on its back. Once this power of words was discovered, the power of saying more than what they were saying, speaking became a risky and exacting operation. I would utter a word, and it was like extending the antenna of a turned-on radio: messages, music, and news descended from the ether. Whatever I said, I was afraid it could be used against me. I would be silent for half an hour before the first undercover word slipped out, like the involuntary flare from an overloaded flashbulb. I'd lie there huddled up, the way a sonogram shows a fetus in the uterus. I protected my guts, the part of me that ached the most. I used my body as though it weren't the body of a man, so deficient in limbs, but that of an octopus, where everything is prehensile, and which shrouds itself to envelop its own umbilicus. But even in this position my hands found it possible to go up right and left along the temples and clench their fingers at the top of my head, just above the nape of the neck.

He interpreted this gesture as a defense to shelter myself from his blows. The rapidity with which he supplied this interpretation suggested to me that he'd used it before: I imagine that everyone going into analysis lies there in the same way. He used the expression "take shelter" and he used the word "blows." The use of these words made his sentence true. If he had said "protect yourself" instead of "take shelter," his sentence would have been false. That all of us should need one word instead of another in order to express the same concept is something that is related to the very essence of man, something in which his history is recapitulated. "Taking shelter" is a fundamental term for me, since I'm of peasant origin, and peasants "take shelter" from storms by running under the porch so as to have something over their heads. They hear the sound of the hail on the roof tiles and say: "It's coming down hard." Therefore "blows" is for me another fundamental word. Fundamental means that it has to do with my foundations, what is deep inside me and on which I base myself: take those words away from me and I'd no longer be able to stand; it would be like removing the columns that support the weight of a cupola. To use another word in place of "shelter," I would first have to undergo a linguistic treatment comparable to brainwashing, an emotional and moral expropriation that would leave me empty and therefore susceptible to new words. I don't say it's an impossible phenomenon: on the contrary, it has happened on a broad scale in Italy, when millions of people were sucked up from the poorer regions toward the richer ones, and obliged to live and speak in a manner different from the one to which they were born. Now whole generations are being thrown back, and on returning to their places of origin speak a strange language that does not keep pace with their souls: like an artificial heart, regulated by transistor, which in moments of anger or stress does not supply a proper flow and leads to cardiac failure. The replacement of the natural heart with an artificial heart is the most important historical event in recent decades. The fact that no newspaper has pointed this out, and all of them talk about other problems, is as though the doctors at the bedside of a cardiac victim were primarily concerned with his hemorrhoids.

My meeting with him became the most important thing in the day, in the week, even (now I find it hard to acknowledge) in life. I postponed all kinds of commitments, involving work, money, and family, so that this fifty-minute hour—plus half an hour to go and half an hour to come back—would be free for our session. If he couldn't keep the appointment, but could on another day, I rearranged my schedule, creating for myself a free hour at the time when he was available. If I wasn't able to free myself, I went to him anyway, and neglected all other obligations.

It could also happen that the whole hour with him would go by without a word being spoken: I would listen to the smell of his tobacco spreading throughout the room and penetrating my body, until the fiftieth minute was up and he would get to his feet, saying, "All right," to indicate that the hour was over. It was an hour spent with him, I was completely penetrated by the smell of his tobacco, and that was enough. Maybe it's homosexual to put it this way since it may suggest a risky relationship . . . I meant to say, maybe it's risky since it may suggest a homosexual relationship. I believe it was not "only" homosexual but much more. A homosexual relationship is an incomplete relationship. Man alone is only a half. One man plus another man do not make two nor do they make one: they make two halves. A man and a woman make one. He and I made one, but we were two men. There was something in this that made our relationship more than homosexual, and more than heterosexual. Perhaps it could be called an omnisexual relationship.

He sat behind me, in a chair provided with armrests, behind a desk. It was a swivel chair. As I took my position on the couch, I imagined him turning the chair toward me, so that when I settled back it was like surrendering myself to him, almost as though I were entering the hollow of his lap and arms. I had the feeling of slipping into that recess like a barge into a harbor. When I was little, I did the same with my mother: I'd go to where she was sitting, turn around, and get into her lap by jumping backwards. My mother bent forward and hugged me. As with my mother, I felt him slowly bending toward me, over me, and once when I turned my head I seemed for a moment to see two breasts descending slowly toward me until they grazed me. Swamped by this vision, I half-closed my eyes and lay there drowsily for the rest of the session. I swallowed slowly. Suddenly, sharp as a cry, I felt the old pain in my nose, which I'd been feeling for years, as though its inner membrane had been pierced by a pin. I didn't move a finger. Without opening my eyes, I turned my face upward, so that my nostrils would be under his nipple, and said or thought: Let just one drop fall on my pain, and my pain will vanish.

9

2. Nasal twinges

No doctor had been able to diagnose this pain in my nose. They said it might be due to local causes or to sudden changes in blood pressure. They smeared my nostrils with hemostatic ointment and prescribed rinsing with a saturated solution of boric acid. I'd pour the solution into the palm of one hand, snort it up one nostril, tilt my head back, and feel the liquid pass from one nostril to the other; when I bent my head forward the water came out of my nose through both nostrils. The nasal cavities were irritated and burned a little. They explained to me that the nose, along with the penis, is the part of a man's body with the most blood vessels. They advised me to have my blood pressure checked at least once a month. I checked it once a week, and I still never knew what it was. I'd look for a pharmacy, wait to calm down before going in, take two Valiums, and walk back and forth for a while looking at store windows until I felt at ease: head clear, blood limpid, nerves sound. I calculated: blood pressure 120. We can go in. I'd go in. My eyes sought out the armchair with the sphygmometer, it's always in a corner, I sat down in it and waited for the pharmacist. The pharmacist glanced at me but continued waiting on customers at the counter. I reviewed my body: head clear, blood tired, nerves weak. I calculated: blood pressure 160. Here's the pharmacist, he's come out from behind the counter without my even noticing, he's here on my left, but why my left? I've already unbuttoned my right sleeve, which is now unnecessary, I also unbutton the left, he binds my arm with the band of the sphygnometer and squeezes the bulb. I review my body: head buzzing, blood chaotic, nerves convulsed. What will my blood pressure be? "Maximum 195." The pharmacist unwound the band from my arm, took a slip of paper and wrote: 27 April, 10:15 a.m., 195 over 90. "Three thousand lire." Leaving the pharmacy, I listened to my body, whose blood pressure stood at almost 200: the blood plugged up my ears, if someone had called me I wouldn't have heard. I walked. Another pharmacy, I look in the door. There's a little old man in the armchair, and the pharmacist is beside him, measuring his blood pressure on the right arm. How high will it be? I look at him: his mouth twitches but his face is serene, his arm doesn't tremble, he has no spots on his skin. I calculate: 140. And I? I review my body: head clear, blood limpid, nerves solid. I calculate: maximum 120. The old man tries to get up but doesn't make it, the pharmacist helps him out of the chair, and then stands there rolling up the sphygmometer. I dash inside and sit down, I already have my right sleeve unbuttoned. The pharmacist is surprised, he unrolls the instrument and wraps my arm. I review my body: head curious, nerves distracted, blood . . . "Maximum 150." He's way ahead of me, he's already written out the slip, and gives it to me: 27 April, 10:50 a.m., 150 over 70. "Three thousand lire." I leave, listening to my body, whose blood pressure stands at 150. It's unclogged, I listen with the right ear and hear perfectly, listen with the left ear and hear perfectly: no one is calling me. I keep walking. Another pharmacy. I enter cheerfully. Where's the sphygmometer? Ah, there it is. I sit down. Someone comes toward me from behind the counter. It's a woman, I hadn't expected such a gesture of courtesy. She wears a tight-fitting white blouse, one can sense the breasts pressing from underneath, right on the tip of the left breast she wears an insignia of the Order of Pharmacists, a large pin, I imagine the fastener of this pin going through the blouse and tickling her nipple. I like this place, I'll always come here to have my blood pressure checked. "Maximum 120." She gives me the slip of paper: 27 April, 11 a.m., 120 over 60. "Three thousand lire." I pay with a five-thousand-lira bill, the lady pharmacist gives me the change, but it wasn't necessary. I go home and line up the slips on the table: 10:15 a.m., pressure in left arm with blood alerted, 195; 10:50 a.m., pressure in right arm with blood surprised, 150; 11 a.m., pressure in right arm with blood distracted by nipple, 120. It's 11:30, I'm not alerted, not surprised, and without the nipple: what will my blood pressure be? Is my nose in danger? I have a headache, and take a Buscopan and an Optalidon.

A pain in the nose is to Buscopan as a splitting headache is to Optalidon, as an ulcer is to Tral, insomnia to Roipnol.

The pain in my nose made me jerk my head back, as though to avoid contact with something. This movement reminded me of an episode that has nothing to do with it. I'll tell it all the same, so that we can then stop thinking about it.

I was still a child, we were all in the courtyard, a hundred, a hundred and fifty people. All sitting or squatting on the ground. Only the Germans were standing up: the German soldiers were kids, sixteen or seventeen years old. They wore very long overcoats, it seemed impossible that they could move their legs in such long overcoats. Each one had a parabellum, I knew what they were called and how they worked, because a few weeks before a German partisan had passed by and asked us for something to drink, I had brought him a flask and a bowl, he filled the bowl and emptied it in three gulps: you could see his Adam's apple going up and down, in and out. To thank me, he took his submachine gun from his shoulder and put it in my hands so I could feel how heavy it was, it was heavy, but maybe for children there are lighter machine guns, then he removed the magazine and rested the stock on my shoulder, he showed me how to grasp the weapon with my left hand under the barrel and my right hand behind the breech. With my index finger I pulled the trigger. The German partisan gave me a slap on the back of the neck and then taught me a trick: he had me push a button from left to right with the thumb of my left hand, and pull the trigger while going "Pow" with my mouth. Then he had me press the button from right to left with the index finger of my left hand, and pull the trigger while going "Tr-r-r-r" with my mouth. I understood in a flash: single shot and rapid fire. It was a parabellum.

Each of those German boy soldiers had his parabellum, but instead of aiming it at us he kept it pointed at the ground or at the sky. They were nice, they didn't want to shoot us. I felt cheerful. A German stood on the road and stopped anyone who passed, he made them get off their bicycles, come in the courtyard, and squat there with the rest of us. Then Uncle Giulio showed up. They had hurt Uncle Giulio, his belly was bleeding from an ugly, blackish hole that he was trying to plug by pressing his shirt over it knotted like a bundle. The hole was low, under the navel. Coming out of that hole, his blood sank lower in his body, and there was none left in his head: his face was completely white. Two Germans were carrying Uncle Giulio, hanging from a pole that passed under his armpits. The Germans walked slowly, to let all of us get a good look at Uncle Giulio's face, but one by one they all shook their heads as he passed, they didn't recognize him, he was too white, they didn't realize what I had realized, that the blood had drained down from his head, there wasn't any left in his head. But still it was he, Uncle Giulio, and when he was in front of me I said to the German who was looking at me, "That's Uncle Giulio." The German smiled at me, he was nice. Uncle Giulio also smiled at me, he was nice too. I smiled at them both, we were friends. The German took his parabellum in his right hand, by the barrel, raised it, and hit my uncle in the face with it. My uncle tried to jerk his head back, but he was stuck on the pole, and the blow caught him right across the nose. His nose was completely white, like flour, but smashed by the blow it began pouring red like the bunghole of a wine cask. My uncle was loaded on a truck, which drove off at full speed. The episode taught me two things: that a pain in the nose makes you jerk your head back, and that there's more blood in an empty nose than wine in a full cask.

Uncle Giulio was very strong. He once lifted a cart out of a ditch and hoisted it back on the road with a push of his shoulders. You could also recognize him by his pants: he always wore pants with a low crotch, as though his balls hung down to his knees. And yet the two German boy soldiers had loaded him on the truck like a sack of potatoes, with no trouble at all: the blow on the nose had put him to sleep.

This is why—it has nothing to do with it, but if I don't say it, I won't be able to get it out of my mind—when you have to take bulls from one stall to another, you lead them by hand, with pincers that you hook onto the nasal septum. The pincers are like a thunderbolt, they discharge volleys of pain all over the body. By pulling this way and that, up and down, you lead the bull as you like, make him kneel and get up—his brain is boiling. The pincers are also used when bulls are castrated to become steers. They are still young bulls, a few months old, but already with a quick jerk of the neck they can snap their iron chains, and once they're free one will jump on the croup of another and try to mount him. No one would pay any attention if it went peacefully and there were homosexual bulls who let themselves be mounted. But all the bulls want to mount and none wants to be mounted.

The mounted bull suddenly escapes by falling on his back on the straw with his belly up; the mounting bull rolls on the fodder with legs spread; the mounted bull straightens up and jumps on the other's back, trying to mount him in his turn, frothing more for revenge than desire; and in this uproar of muttering and chains rattling and doors being smashed and horns broken, the nights, weeks, and months go by, until at the end of the first year the gelder arrives with the iron pincers made in the shape of a large nutcracker, and placing himself behind the first bull he seizes one of his balls with the pincers and begins to squeeze: the bull becomes a steer, from a steer he becomes a lamb, from a lamb a chick, you can stroke him, take him in hand, curry him, put burning medicine on his wounds, scratch his dewlaps. The pincers crush the ball and make the juice come out. The bull gives a sob, he lies there breathless on the straw, and his eyes are red as though full of blood. He is no longer a bull.

I never found out what the Germans did to Uncle Giulio.

3. The cat bite

He was a heavy smoker, cigarettes or pipe, and his consulting room was always saturated with the smell of tobacco. Pipe tobacco is stronger than that of cigarettes, and its smell is a pungent and stimulating perfume, like certain Oriental aromas. At the beginning of my hour, as soon as he was seated, I could hear him searching among his papers for his smoking implements, unscrewing the stem of his pipe, removing the filter and blowing into it, screwing it back, scraping the inside of the bowl, pouring in tiny spoonfuls of tobacco, tamping it down with the proper tool, and then, in an always identical and unmistakable ritual, starting to light the pipe with matches or his cigarette lighter. He never succeeded with the first try. He used up at least three matches, or clicked the lighter at least three times.

These preparations transmitted to me a restless satisfaction or a subtle discomfort: it depended on whether I had nothing with which to begin (in which case I would beg silently: Don't light up, I have nothing to say) or had a dream or episode or idea that I wanted to come out with immediately (Hurry up, I'm ready). In the early sessions I wanted the preparations never to end, and the analysis, which I had been so keen on, and for which I'd been on his waiting list for two years, to be postponed indefinitely.

Indeed, in the first session, I had wanted the whole

17

hour to go by with neither he nor I assuming analytical positions. I had remained standing by the window, he was seated at his desk with his hands flat on the surface and his pipe in his mouth. He was smoking and had a faint smile on his lips. He was waiting for me to move. I pushed aside the curtain and looked out. There was a cat on the window, and there were three or four others in the courtyard. Only a minute before the hour ended did I move away from the window and lie down on the couch: in time so it could be said to have happened but with no time left for it to be discussed. He looked at me and said immediately, "All right." We got up and he walked me to the door.

I was always astonished by the number of cats that collected around his house, drowsy, crouching with heavy eyelids, and sometimes stretched out on the ground.

Once—it was one of the early sessions but not the first—I found one of these cats on the third step leading up to the door of the house. It was warming itself in a lingering ray of sunlight. It was white, big, obese. It was in my way. Partly for this reason, and partly to have friendly relations (at least with a cat, since he never answered my questions), I put out my hand to stroke its neck. With eyes half closed, the cat lazily watched my hand approach, and when it was within range it arched its back and . . . bit my forefinger. It didn't scratch it with its claws, it bit it with its teeth, like a dog. It was the right hand. Stunned, I stared at my hand, which was bleeding copiously. I looked at my watch: my hour began in one minute. I waited a minute (I insisted, I still insist, on being punctual, and if I have to make an appointment I never say, for example, "at 8:30," but "at

8:32," and that way the other party knows not to be late), and then I rang the bell, a short ring, as always. I heard a door open inside, then slam shut: he was coming up toward me, leaving behind his wife (did he have a wife?), or children (did he have children?), or parents (did he live with his parents?), he was coming forward, dragging his feet, he was here, he was mine. He turned the latch, opened the door, and smiled. I walked up my three steps. At his level, I raised my hand, put my finger before his eyes, and said, "Your cat . . . it bit me."

The smile retreated from his lips but did not vanish altogether. He looked at my finger and looked at the cat. "I'll take care of it right away," he said. "It's not my cat."

He turned and disappeared in the hallways of his house. He came back with a wad of cotton, a bottle of hydrogen peroxide (I was expecting painless alcohol, or better still, penicillin ointment), and adhesive tape. I dabbed my finger with hydrogen peroxide, wiped it with the cotton, covered it with adhesive tape, and held it with my left hand. Once this was done, we could proceed. I felt more secure than usual, now he owed me something, or to put it better, now he too was at fault.

For the whole hour I talked about various things, fairly freely, and almost cheerfully, if there can be said to be a minute of cheerfulness in years of analysis.

For some reason or other, just as I was leaving, in addition to the usual *arrivederci* (which he, not being from the Veneto, pronounced by fully sounding the *c*), I said, "We covered just about everything today."

He blinked his eyes, looked at the bandaged finger, and replied, "That got left out."

19

It was true. An event so important in our relations (blood had flowed), and not a word had been said about it.

Never again did I pet his cats. I tried to be punctual to the second, I arrived and rang the bell, he opened the door and I went in.

As soon as I was inside I would check with a glance to see whether he had his implements and little bag of tobacco on the desk (today he's smoking a pipe), or if instead there was nothing (today he's smoking cigarettes). His brand was Muratti. I would wait for him to light up: one, two, three strikes, it's lit. Now the first puff. The session had begun.

4. The tax evader

Analysis looks like a situation of absolute freedom: you can say whatever comes into your head. Actually analysis is a situation of absolute constraint: in it you can only say what you say, because you don't have anything else to say. Persons who go into analysis gravitate around the analyst for three or eleven years, describing orbits one of whose foci is occupied by the analyst (the other focus is occupied by the persons reincarnated by the analyst); they can cut loose and return to earth, they can go on gravitating indefinitely until the friction consumes them, they can break out of the orbit and lose themselves in the spaces of madness. But whatever happens, the result is the exact consequence of the relation between the forces in the field: things can go only the way they go.

There are moments when analysis is a risk: it can go well, it can go badly. There are moments when analysis is a danger: it can only go badly. The first situation is constant. The second is intermittent.

Since there are no dead areas in analysis, the attempts made not with him but with others, when he was unavailable, didn't have time, or didn't want me, also form part of my analysis. My relationship with him was indeed an achievement, and it took years. My relationship with the others was as easy and pointless as a relationship with a call girl: it could be arranged by telephone. You call up, and the wife or son answers, tells you he's not there, he's at the hospital, he'll be back at two in the afternoon, if you like he'll get back to you. So you know he's married to a housewife, has a son who doesn't go to school, works at the hospital, has chosen to work part time (meaning that he earns 1,400,000 lire), and will call back, introduce himself, and say, "This is Dr. So-and-so returning your call, what can I do for you?" When you know all this, you already know too much, it no longer makes sense to undertake an analysis. You can go if you like, like someone who sets out to see a movie, but when he gets to the theater finds that the one he wanted to see isn't playing anymore: as long as he's there, he might as well go in, but he knows beforehand that he won't be seeing his film and will probably leave before it's half over. Thus for a few months I went to someone in Venice who was quite unlike him. There was a telephone on his table, and every so often it rang.

"Excuse me a minute," he'd say to me as he lifted the receiver and answered: "Yes . . . after five . . . all right, six o'clock . . . fifteen thousand . . . your name, please? . . . don't worry, we'll look into that too"—exactly the way a call girl, in the middle of intercourse, lifts the telephone receiver and is already thinking of her next customer:

"Hold still, honey," she says to you, and to the phone: "Yes . . . morning or evening, whichever you like . . . all right, this evening . . . no, right now I have somebody else . . . fifteen thousand . . . we can do that too, that's thirty thousand."

Analysis is a little like a space trip. You're there wait-

ing to get into orbit, and he's using the ship's transmit-
ter to talk to someone who's completely extraneous.
Many trips fail for this reason, and fleets of space ships
wander through the galaxies, and now speak only
among themselves. The analyst's success depends less
on what he knows than on what he is.

It would be hard to go further wrong than with the
doctor in Venice. His office was so full of his presence
that there was no room for anyone else. He would
sneeze, sniffle when he blew his nose, and while you
were talking he'd twiddle his thumbs, fiddle with papers, open and close books. There you were, with that
knot in your guts (choked up like a clogged pipe), and
he's picking his nose. He's waiting for you to speak. But
doesn't he understand? Isn't he aware that I express
myself with silence, breathing, sighing, crossing my
legs, scratching my forehead three times a minute, and
every time I lower my hand I touch my nose because of
the piercing pain inside?

Words cannot say what silence says. The most intense
and most useful hours of my true analysis were the
"blank" hours, without a word on my part or his. His
silence was so total that I had the impression, and sometimes the certainty, that he'd left the room. Then after
half an hour, I'd hear the faint tap of his forefinger on
his cigarette, and even imagine I could hear the ashes
dropping into the ashtray. So he was there.

Silence is full of sounds. In the most total silence, in
the course of a blank hour, you suddenly feel a twinge
in the cartilage of your nose and remove your hand from
the nape of your neck to scratch it. Lifting the hand

disturbs the body, and every small part of the body produces its own sound, from the hair freed from your fingers to the shoes that you've been resting on each other. He hears these sounds, distinguishes and follows them. Just like an acoustical technician trying to analyze a sound, he says, "You moved your feet, do you want to leave?"

Or: "You're looking for something with your hands."

Or: "Something is making you sigh."

Gradually, as the years go by, you learn that when there are so many interpretations, you don't have to choose the true one and discard the others: if each explains something, they're all true. You went into analysis in order to discover the reason why you entered analysis, and in the end you discover that there was not a single reason, but two or three, three or four, four or five thousand. Every day of your life, starting even before you were born, has contributed a hundred or so: now you must walk backwards and get rid of them. At a certain point in your life, those reasons began reproducing themselves, they no longer needed any help from outside. Now you must set in motion corrective mechanisms that will in their turn reproduce themselves. And this operation is called analysis.

The doctor in Venice did not have this conception of analysis. For him, speech in analysis was like any other kind of speech: if one asks a question, the other is obliged to supply an answer; if the phone rings, one lifts the receiver and answers it; since the analysis is taking place in his house where his family also lives, his family constantly intrudes on your analysis and besieges it, you hear his children running in the hallway, their mother scolding them, the maid using the vacuum cleaner (no analyst should have a vacuum cleaner in his house, and every analyst ought to be subject to an approval rating by his patients over the years). This is the kind of analyst who calls you at home to say: "Oh, I forgot to tell you, tomorrow I'll be in Milan all day for a convention, so we'll have to cancel our appointment."

To cancel an appointment is one of the most effective means for relaunching the analysis, since it produces a situation of abandonment that re-evokes all the times you've been abandoned in life.

But this departure of the Venetian doctor re-evokes nothing, it's an isolated instance: you know he's the one who's going away, you know he's going to a convention, going to Milan, leaving in the morning and coming back in the evening. It's not a symbol, it's a fact.

The Venetian doctor preferred to conduct the analysis from armchair to armchair, which meant that his sluggish, stocky body was constantly in front of me, like a landslide on a road. He was big and fat, with a body that constantly made noise (rumbling, gurgling, growling in the stomach, belches and burps), causing him serious embarrassment and obliging him always to invent ways to cover up these sounds and conceal them: he kept coughing, moving books, riffling papers.

These snags also occurred because he was available in the early hours of the afternoon, just after the midday meal, and indeed his fits of coughing diffused in the room a strong odor of coffee, like steam from a coffee pot. For an hour I was immersed in the effluvia from his digestion.

After I'd been going to him for three or four months, I had a dream: I dreamt that my armchair, while I was seated in it, started stretching itself, and the back kept going down, down, until it became a bed. I, who had been sitting in that armchair, facing the analyst, now found myself stretched out on that bed, alone. Then I realized that something in me was refusing to continue this armchair analysis, and wanted another analysis, with the couch.

I told this decision to the analyst, paid him for the whole month even though we were only in the first week, and left. Before walking me to the door, he wrote out a receipt for me, but put down on it only half of what I had actually paid him. "Like everyone else," he explained, "I cheat on my taxes," and laughed.

Come to think of it, that says it all.

He had handled my analysis the way a worker at Fiat does his overtime, and welcomed my decision to break off the relationship exactly the way a house painter responds to a reduction in his work schedule: with a combination of annoyance and satisfaction, annoyance because his earnings are diminished, satisfaction because he has less work to do.

5. The orgy

Having begun in Venice, my journey into wild analysis shifted to Rome. I live in Padua. Rome is to the south. Ever since then I find it unbearable to travel south—for me it foretells failure. Man is a fly caught in a cobweb of symbols, and every time he makes a movement the whole cobweb is shaken.

The doctor in Rome analyzed individually, but selected his patients by summoning them in groups. These group receptions were like the aptitude tests given by company psychologists. Many are called but few are chosen, and those few are assigned different destinies: some two hours a week, some three, some four, some five. Even the fees are different, and are in proportion to the patient's income: each pays for an hour what he earns in an hour. Moreover, those who are excluded are not wholly rejected, but are allowed to attend group-analysis sessions, twice a week. No one knows on what basis the doctor in Rome makes his selections: they all show up together, speak as they like (generally one at a time, according to precedence or proximity to the doctor), say what they like, and he decides at once whether he will take them or not, for how many hours, and on which days. Behind him a secretary writes it all down. You can't argue about anything, object, or ask for an explanation. It's just not done.

A girl student ahead of me introduced herself by her

first name (no one ever gave his or her surname, and the first names by themselves left an impression of total anonymity), and offered a case of what she called "loss of identity." The professor (it made no difference to this analyst in Rome whether you called him doctor or professor) nodded as though he'd already understood, actually the girl student didn't mean "loss of identity" at all, and indeed she corrected herself immediately, saying "loss of interest," the professor nodded again, she said that even if her mother died she wouldn't give a damn. The professor nodded.

"Three hours," he said. "Monday, Tuesday, and Saturday at 11 a.m."

The girl informed him that she had a class on Monday and asked if she could switch to Wednesday. The professor smiled sadly, with a resigned look, and bowed his head. His secretary stopped writing and looked at the troublemaker. The whole group—some sixty persons, almost all of them quite young—turned toward the girl with a questioning look. There was a moment of total silence. The girl bowed her head and repeated, in a low voice:

"Monday . . . Tuesday . . . Saturday, at 11 a.m."

She looked around apologetically and went out. The group felt immediately relieved, and showed it by a rising murmur.

The incident made a huge impression, because it made palpable the fact that analysis stands above everything else, so far above that it cannot be measured or compared with anything else. Where analysis is there's no room for anything else. When you're in analysis, all else is in abeyance.

My turn having come, I made a very brief presentation, impersonal and insincere, speaking as though I were someone else talking about me. As I spoke, I could see the professor's lips continually moving, as though they were being simultaneously worked by the smiling muscles and the crying muscles. It was a nervous tic that made his cheeks twitch persistently as well. Suddenly he raised his hand and brushed aside a lock of hair that kept falling stubbornly in front of his eyes; in so doing, he tossed his head, a quick motion, careless and natural, of the kind made by women. Indeed, there was something feminine about him. He wore dark glasses, like Garbo. He never looked anyone in the face, but he felt that everyone was looking at him.

I cut short my speech as soon as I could, even before it made complete sense.

He seemed surprised, undoubtedly he hadn't been listening to me, and was thinking of something else. Suddenly he turned to look at me and blushed. He didn't know what to decide. Lips trembling, between laughter and tears, he said, "Thursday and Saturday, 2 p.m."

It was rather early for me. To be there at two in the afternoon I'd no longer be able to leave at dawn, but would have to leave the night before. It was, however, the last private session, the group session began immediately thereafter, and so I couldn't request a later appointment. I accepted, or rather it was so obvious that I had to accept that I said nothing, and stayed on for a while longer to watch a few other selections.

Next came a woman in her thirties, dark-skinned and dark-haired, short and fat, with her hair falling in front

29

of her face like a curtain, which prevented her from seeing and being seen. She took one or two steps forward. None of us had done that: each had spoken from his or her place. But she had this need, to advance into the void, like an object being displayed in isolation at an auction in order to be appraised.

A boy, behind her, kept both his hands on her shoulders; it was he who was pushing her forward and guiding her steps, since she could see nothing and under the cover of her hair was crying softly, sucking in her tears with the corners of her mouth. It was the boy who spoke.

"Pia," he said in a gentle voice, seeking sympathy, "can't get over the idea that she's fat . . ."

"But she *is* fat," the professor interrupted unexpectedly. All eyes turned to him, and you could see that on his lips, gripped by the irrepressible tic, the impulse to smile nevertheless prevailed. Everybody smiled, a few laughed.

"She doesn't go out of the house," continued the boy, who was smiling too, as though he had gone over to the side of the group, "and she's stopped attending classes, she's missed three finals; she keeps studying but won't take exams."

"And what more does she want?" laughed the professor. Others laughed, including the boy. Everybody laughed, but politely, and then—incredibly—the girl started laughing too, although she didn't stop crying. She was gasping, and her tears fell by fits and starts.

The professor got to his feet. The meeting was over. They all remained seated without making any noise, exchanging papers and books, opening and closing briefcases, saying their goodbyes, and hugging each other. The professor adjusted his blind man's dark glasses on his nose, tossed back his hair with a flick of hand and head, descended from the platform, and started toward the door. Then something happened that I hadn't foreseen, that couldn't have been foreseen. Whenever I try to imagine something both simple and extraordinary, it is the professor's progress from the platform to the exit that comes to mind. For him to be able to take those few steps, the crowd had to make way for him. The crowd did indeed make way, but not enough to allow him to pass freely: he lowered one foot into the small empty space that opened before him; in lowering it he touched knees, ankles, briefcases, jeans, hands; he drew up the other foot and moved it forward to occupy another small niche that had opened in the meantime, and he did all this cautiously, so as to touch everyone and not hurt anyone. It was ten or twelve steps from platform to door, and the time it took him was out of proportion to the distance, while he kept smiling sadly, his tearful smile, which gradually faded until at the end it was nothing but pure grief. He lifted his feet and set them down the way Alpine troops lift their boots and set them down on the snow; the people around him would have liked to become snow, to be touched, trampled, crushed. Finally he reached the door. At the door stood two clusters of students, leaving a small crack between them. He turned his body sideways and edged through the crack: he went out scraping both sides, like a sheep making its way between two thorn bushes and leaving tufts of wool on every thorn. Once he had got through, people moved away from the door, and the crowd split up into groups, with everyone smiling and touching and hugging each other, boys with girls, boys with boys, girls with girls, as though each had received something and wanted to share it with the others, or feared that the others had received something and was hoping to become part of it. The fat girl had parted her curtain of hair, holding it aside with both hands, and was looking all around. Her lips were dry, feverish, slightly gaping. She had stopped crying.

6. The thieving friar

To be in Rome by early afternoon I used to take the midnight train. I'd reserve a berth, always a lower since I knew I wouldn't get any sleep and ought to allow myself the possibility of going out in the corridor. Incredible as it seems, every time you go to Rome, whether day or night, first or second class, you run into a priest or friar. At night this priest or friar is usually lodged in the upper berth: he has light and air there, and is closer to God. Lying on his back, completely dressed (his cassock is like a dressing gown anyway), holding his breviary with both hands, he prays uninterruptedly in a very subdued voice but not in silence, and at every page he makes the sign of the cross. It was by looking at these sleepless, oracular, weak, babbling priests and friars that I realized we had something in common, they and I, and it was precisely the thing that kept us up all night and—a curious fact, charged with meanings that I'll never succeed in getting to the bottom of—for which we were going to Rome. This thing established a relationship between me and them, between us and the night, us and sleep, and us and Rome. Of course, if I made these discoveries about them, they made the same ones about me. But perhaps here the truth is more subtle, and more difficult to express. I had the feeling that once I had made a discovery, that discovery was now made and was one discovery less that man had to make: having just made that discovery, I was no longer what I was before, and the way I behaved in the compartment (staying awake, going out or coming back, putting on or taking off a sweater, lying down or sitting up) was that of a person who involuntarily says: I'm not alone, there's someone here like me. Then the other's behavior changes too, because whatever he does (turning a page, making a pause, speeding up his beads, making the sign of the cross over a new page, snuffling, screening the light with a sheet of paper), he does with the involuntary thought: That fellow says I'm like him. But how do I resemble him?

A friar in the same cell with another friar doesn't put a screen in front of the light, there no need for it, it would be an insult. After a while, the friar in my compartment would give me a look and remove the sheet of paper from the light. There is something that relates neurosis to religion. There is something that relates religion to neurosis. I'm not saying that religion is a neurosis, but that neurosis is a form of religion: it has its mysteries, its rites, its obsessions, its taboos, and imposes its own life style. Not only that, but what comes before and after neurosis is what comes before and after religion: upstream, an immense guilt; downstream, an endless expiation. For the whole night, every night, on all those trains, I was expiating, and so were those friars. But I was suffering, and they weren't. If they slept for a quarter of an hour, on reawakening they were repentant, disheartened, and frantic; if I slept a little, on reawakening I was astonished and consoled. Religion is the admission of guilt and the desire for expiation. Neurosis is ignorance of guilt and resistance to expiation. Religion is peace, neurosis conflict.

Traveling by train at night isn't like traveling by train during the day, not only because there's no daylight, but also because the train is different and so are the passengers. Traveling by train at night has something to do with war, and the train is a troop train. The conductors circulate through the cars, they take your documents and keep them until dawn, and if you go out in the corridor they stare at you and try to remember who you are. The passengers (workers, emigrants, and commuters) circulate like patrols, the conductors keep to themselves like snipers. When the snipers go to sleep, the patrols spread out through the train as in a no-man's land. No passenger therefore sleeps soundly at night. So I was never alone in my insomnia. Everyone kept me company by turns, now one, now another; the priest or friar always kept me company. We shared the same sickness.

Boarding the train at midnight, I could enter the compartment without concern, nobody is yet asleep at that hour, they've all been kept awake by the novelty of the journey (they've just got on, at Trieste or Venice), or if they're foreigners, by the curiosity that always arouses you the minute you cross a frontier. I would enter half asleep, with my limbs all disjointed and heavy with the day's toxins. I'd slide my suitcase into a corner, take off my shoes, and stretch out on my back. Finally I could sleep, eight hours. But as though I'd swallowed a pep pill, my sleepiness slowly vanished, my brain purified itself of slag, my fingers and toes moved constantly, my insides swelled beneath my navel and bumped against the skin of my stomach like animals trying to jump out. I spread my warm hands over them, palms down. I looked around. And there in the semidarkness by his shaded light the friar turned, scrutinized me for a moment with a pair of sharp little eyes, and seemed to say to me: But *I* have found a solution.

But let's not drag things out. Let's get to the point. If I've talked about friars and priests, there's another reason for it: I was robbed by a friar or a priest. It was around the third or fourth month, one Wednesday night. I'd fallen asleep for a moment on my stomach, and I had my wallet in the back pocket of my jeans. How it happened that I'd turned over, I don't know, maybe the better to warm my insides. I must have fallen asleep as the train was reaching the outskirts of Florence. Until then I had prowled through the corridors and toilets, amid drafts of gelid air, like a dying cat looking for a place to hide. Approaching Florence, I began shivering with cold and fever. In the toilet mirror I tried vainly to inspect my tonsils, which felt swollen and painful when I swallowed. I retired to my compartment (everyone was asleep, including the friar, how healthy they were!), and curled up in my berth, wrapping myself in the blanket. I woke up a little past Florence, the train was going through a series of Apennine tunnels, at a steady speed, with no variations, as though they had put it on automatic pilot. As we passed a small rural station, a ray of light filtered into the compartment, and I saw at once— for I instinctively sought out the traveling companion who resembled me: was he sleeping? praying? reading?—I saw that the friar was no longer there: the berth empty, the blanket in a heap, one edge of it dangling.

Ah-ha, I thought, with a flash of satisfaction, he's in the toilet.

But instinctively I place my hand on the back pocket of my pants, and it feels flat. I put my hand inside and it's empty. Calmly I realize that something new has occurred, something that creates a practical problem for me: they've stolen my wallet. Oddly enough, very odd indeed, my first thought is: A good thing they robbed me when I was going and not when I was coming back. This thought contains a plan: I must talk about it with the professor. This plan depends on one condition: I must be sure they've robbed me. I look under the berth, and stick my hand in the cracks between the frame and the headboard: nothing. Now it's certain, I've been robbed, I don't have a lira. Well, well, well.

All the others lie there sleeping noisily, there's not one that doesn't snore, and only the friar is missing. Aching all over, I drag myself out of the berth. I open the door and look out into the corridor, the sniper-conductor is sitting there at the end of the car, awake. And yet the thieving friar could only have passed that way. So everything is in order. The thieving friar got off at Florence because that's where he had to get off. He's gone. Well, well, well.

Finally we get to Rome. It's eight-fifteen in the morning. I should eat breakfast but I can't. In six hours I must be at the professor's, there's a tram that runs from here to there but I can't take it. I set out on foot. Usually I check my suitcase, but this time I can't. The status of a man without money is revealed to me for what it is: he's nothing.

But let's not drag things out. Let's get to the point. If

I've talked about the theft, there's another reason for it: the way the professor dealt with the matter.

Of course, I spoke about it immediately, it was my problem. But the professor immediately looked annoyed, and his lips, always wavering between smiling and tears, gave way to disgust.

He tapped both ends of his cigarette on the table, stuck it in his mouth, lit it with the first strike, inhaled, puffed, pushed his knee against the desk, leaned back in his chair, and demanded point-blank, "How much did they steal from you?"

I hadn't expected that. I didn't know. Usually I started out with a hundred thousand lire, but hoped to spend much less. "A hundred thousand lire," I replied.

He inhaled again, and holding the cigarette between forefinger and middle finger, rested his palm on the edge of the desk. "And how much do you need?" he asked.

As I say, I always spent much less than I brought, because I economize on everything, and because I don't feel safe without a reserve. So I replied, "Half."

Here something happened that I didn't expect. I'll never forget it if I live to be a thousand. He inhaled once more, took the cigarette between thumb and middle finger, reached for the ashtray, tapped the cigarette three times with his forefinger, put it down on the edge, opened a drawer, and—I swear—took out five ten-thousand-lira bills, put them in an envelope, and handed it to me.

"That takes care of the theft," he said. "Let's talk about something else."

7. *Electric shocks*

To the patient the analyst is an unknown quantity. This unknowing state is the preliminary condition of analysis: it provides a reason for it.

Our memories are like a film that has been developed; analysis is a double exposure: one re-uses the same film, photographing the new images of analysis over the old images of life. In holding a twice-exposed film up to the light, you're no longer able to make out what it shows, you can't tell the analyst's nose from your father's. It's a family portrait but for some reason there's someone else in it. Analysis exists precisely because there is this riddle to be solved. If the riddle isn't there, no analysis takes place.

By giving me money, the professor in Rome solved this riddle and made it impossible. Holding the film of my life up to the light, I could no longer have any doubts: that one there, with his bundle of fifty thousand lire, was the analyst, it couldn't be anyone else. My family group did not have an extra member. My family members were on one side and the analyst on the other. The double exposure had failed. The same thing happens with cameras: you wanted the second photo to be superimposed on the first, and instead the second photo didn't come out; the first photo is there and that's all. For me, my Roman experience, or rather Rome, represented this blank, this deficiency. The professor gave me back half the money stolen from me on my trip, but he took away from me any reason to make that trip. And in a certain sense he knew he was taking something away from me, and for this reason he gave me money: by reimbursing me, he was identifying with the thief.

Since, as I said, my hour was the last hour of private analysis before the group session, I lived every minute in terror of a sudden invasion by the crowd. I kept an ear cocked, listening to the footsteps and voices, and imagining the gestures, of whoever was on the other side of the door, and trying to figure out whether it was just one person, or three or four, by now perhaps forty or fifty, or all of them. Of course, to get the most out of my trips, I also stayed for the group sessions. Thus I spent eight hours coming, eight in Rome, plus another eight going back, for a bit of individual analysis plus two or three hours (no limit was set) of group analysis. This produced total confusion in my mind, and nevertheless it was beneficial, since it left no room for anything else, occupied everything, and thus also banished my problems, made my symptoms subside, and dissolved my anxieties. I was able to verify this phenomenon in all the others: they were so rarely sad that they could be called happy, but their happiness was ever so slightly muffled. They moved as in limbo, and I with them. Each of them, during those hours, delved into his own dreams and those of the others, took possession of the unconscious of others, shouldered everyone's problems, and thus depersonalized re-emerged into the world, took the tram, and went home or to work or to visit friends. After three or four months of this bath in the group's unconscious, I was so transformed that I couldn't have cared less if they'd stolen my wallet, or even robbed all the cars on the train. It had nothing to do with me, I was somewhere else.

Those three Roman hours were like a hot bath, luke-warm to boiling, that lulls you into lethargy and puts you to sleep. You sleep, and the world goes its own way.

There are soccer teams that as part of their training submerge themselves in boiling hot tubs before every game: it helps make their muscles elastic. While the players are there, in water up to their chins, the coach stands on the edge and releases a series of small electric shocks, which produce a momentary contraction of the heart and other muscles, followed by relaxation. The players feel themselves loosened and made resilient all together, contracted all together, relaxed all together: they are no longer so many bodies and minds, but a single multiform body and a single collective mind. The same was true of us. Every so often our torpor received an electric shock that went through all of us. And since I'm about to give you a few examples, I feel I ought first to mention that there was a priest among us. There, I've told you. I'm not sure why.

The group sessions did not form a cycle, they did not start on a particular date and end after a certain length of time: God knows when they'd begun, and they would go on for the rest of the professor's life. His name was Bartolomeo, but everyone called him Bart and used the familiar *tu*, with the same devotion with which the wor-shipper addresses his God as "thou": "Our Father who art in heaven . . ." Whoever entered this group analysis was suddenly dropped into a tangle of relations that had years of history behind it. Like a soccer player arriving late for training who gets hit by an electric shock as soon as he gets in the tub.

"Bart," a girl began at the first session; she was in her twenties, I think, but I can't say for sure, since I was in the back row and saw everyone from behind; they pronounced Bart by drawling the *a*: "Baart, last night I had a dream, and it seemed to me that I'd finally overcome my frigidity, because a finger kept stroking my clitoris and I liked it, and it wasn't my own finger, although it wasn't my boy friend's finger either, and anyway I was happy, and just lay there with my legs spread."

"It was my finger," the professor replied instantly, "and when I make love, I don't like it if the woman just lies there—that to me is frigidity. I don't say she has to squirm and moan like an actress in a porn film, but she should move a little, she should push back. You never move, Lidia, you lie there in front of me with your legs spread, but you never push back. Spreading your legs is a sign of readiness but not of participation."

The shock hit the priest and the new arrivals; the veterans absorbed it like a caress: their muscles were more flexible. Lidia closed her legs a little, but immediately opened them again.

"Baart," began another girl, from the corner near the door, "last night I dreamt I was in an oasis in the desert, and I felt fine there, and so I turned away the camels that somebody had sent to get me. I was in the shade and there was water, and I was watching this line of camels coming toward me and I sent them back, so these camels were coming by one path and going back by another parallel path, and I watched carefully and counted the camels with my finger, because I was terrified that I'd miss one and it would stay in my oasis, where there was shade and water."

"I see," said the professor, laughing and crying. "Giovanna doesn't want me to make her pregnant, and that's why she's terrified. But I won't make her pregnant by violence—I've never raped anyone. Some have raped me, like Carla last week. You line up my spermatozoa and send them back, and you're careful not to let any of them enter your oasis (it's been called by different names, but to tell the truth, this is the most poetic one, especially if we try to see it from the point of view of my poor camels, who've crossed the desert to get inside and enjoy that shade and water), you're afraid that even a single one of my camels will get in and hide in your shady, moist oasis, because you might get pregnant. But if Giovanna won't let herself get pregnant by me," concluded the professor, looking around the whole room, "how will we be able to have a child together?"

"Those camels arrived straight and left crooked, staggering. I was afraid they'd die in the desert," continued Giovanna, who wanted to tell the end of her dream.

"You thought there was no other oasis for them but your own. You have a divine conception of your oasis, the same conception that my camels must have had of it. But this also terrifies you: if they don't get into your oasis, what can the camels do except die? To free you from your terror, I can tell you that everyone dies in the desert"— he had his crying mouth—"except camels, and that there's always more than one oasis, you just have to find them." He smiled. Everyone smiled, a few laughed. The priest and the new arrivals (they, we, were the farthest from the professor; proximity had to be earned with time) received new shocks, a few of them fatal: if they withstood them, they could go on with the training; otherwise they would either disappear or end up on the sidelines, among the fans, custodians, and sports writers. The schools of analysis have limited teams but hordes of fans.

"Baart"—it was a male voice—"I dreamt I went to work at the hospital at an unscheduled hour, I'm a psychiatrist, and the nun in charge of the department, her name is Teresa, was holding the money for my fee, as though it had been a regular assignment."

"Give your earnings back to the hospital. You can't work part-time," commanded the professor. The electric shocks were not the same for everyone: this one was experienced as fatal only by the psychiatrist, by the others it wasn't even noticed. The priest, turning toward the psychiatrist, kept nodding his head, as if he, having just survived two fatal shocks, was fully in agreement with the professor, who had twice tried to strike him down. The room was continually dividing and composing itself according to sudden and instinctive alliances, born perhaps by chance but destined to last for a lifetime. Alliances perhaps even closer than those uniting parents with children, brothers with brothers. No sooner had Lidia, the frigid girl, ceased speaking than another girl left the back of the room, carrying along her stool and lifting it high above the heads of the participants, and moved next to Lidia, where she carved out a spot for herself. Now they sat huddled together and talking: two frigid girls, or two lesbians, beginning a relationship that, so I imagined, would never end.

Other connections had been forged before, and in fact the ranks of the participants were subdivided into groups, formed to unite around the same problem. As I gradually discovered, a new and unforeseen phenomenon accordingly took place, the most striking feature of this collective analysis: each subgroup gathered around a problem, the leadership within the subgroup was held by whoever embodied that problem to the highest degree, and the progress of the group was measured by the progress of its leader. The Thursday leaders were Lidia, Giovanna, Gabriella, Giorgio, and Fabio. There were other leaders on Saturday. If a leader couldn't come on Thursday, he or she came on Saturday, and all or almost all the members of the group switched to Saturday. Then something paradoxical, but inevitable in this kind of experiment, happened: the leaders were problem-persons, sickness-persons; the groups were sickness-groups. The absence of a group leader meant the absence of a sickness, and the rise of a group leader meant the introduction of a new sickness.

The first day I attended, the sicknesses and groups represented by the leaders were Frigidity, Money, Menstruation, Death, Inferiority, Masturbation, and Abandonment; the second day they were Impotence, Castration, the Only Child, the Male Breast, the Woman's Penis, the Undersized Penis, Death, and Abandonment. Death and Abandonment came on both Thursday and Saturday (it's not analysis if it doesn't confront the fear of Death and Abandonment, since there is no problem of man that is not the problem of Death, of which the problem of Abandonment forms part). The shifting of the Death and Abandonment groups never disturbed the analysis, on the contrary, it enriched it with new insights; those who were afraid of dying if they took a train could meet with those who were afraid of dying if they stayed home, and so while the first group analyzed the anxiety dream of a train journey (the train a rattlesnake, the cars its rattle), you saw the other group withdraw into a deadly silence, hang on every syllable, every sound, every detail of the dream and its symbols, and you felt that every brain was wondering: How come these people have the same anxiety starting from an opposite cause? This helped the analysis; it made it clear that between point of departure (house, train) and point of arrival (anxiety, death) there was no relation of cause and effect; to think so was deceiving, it was a trick of one's sickness; the relation was between symptom and symbol.

Thursday's problems—Frigidity, Money, Menstruation, Inferiority, Masturbation, Death, and Abandonment—ended by becoming one huge single problem. Each had his or her own particular problem, but it became somewhat contaminated by the problems of others. Thus someone who had the problem of Death began after months to recover from the Menstruation problem, which he had never had; and someone who had come because of Money after a while found himself to have the Frigidity problem too, and God knows what else. It was as though sailors infected with plague or cholera were to be put aboard a ship being quarantined for smallpox: after a while, those with smallpox start worrying particularly about choleraic dysentery, and if they survive that, they consider themselves cured. In analysis and in neurosis (analogous situations) the vehicle of contagion is the word. The word of the neurotic, of the analysand, and of the analyst performs the same function as the word of the poet: it fosters seduction and produces imitation. Since the word came from the leaders of the sickness groups, the seduction was due to their example, which was also the goal for the attempted imitation: after a month or so, all the members of a group deteriorated to the level of the group leader, after which they began laboriously to climb back. The arrival of a new leader, group, or sickness then provoked a crisis of rejection: there was an immediate effort to shunt it aside, keep it in isolation, enclose it within the barbed wire of silence, deny it any surface or underground contact. As though that quarantined ship were to be boarded by a crew of tuberculars, and they were to be told: Take two cabins, a latrine, and a galley, and stay put. If at a session on Frigidity, Money, Inferiority, and Abandonment, a representative of Castration or the Woman's Penis tried to speak up, all the participants closed ranks, denied him the floor, refused to listen to his questions, and kept themselves immune while wondering: What germ is he carrying? What sickness does it produce? Has it already attacked me? What treatment should I take? On that quarantined ship, anyone who has cholera asks himself at his first boil whether he doesn't also have the plague, and no one will be able to assure him that he doesn't.

To avoid contact with the newcomer, it was enough not to get into conversation with him: the word could pass only from him to the analyst and back to him, without touching the group. But the suspicion of contagion had already been born, and it died hard. If some listless person seemed unable to move his fingers, everybody wondered: Do my fingers move all right? He can't manage a tongue twister. Let's try she-sells-seashells . . . He hears a buzzing in his right ear. How's my hearing? Should I buy an audiometer? Go to an ear, nose, and throat doctor? Neurosis is an expiation. Since all sufferings provide fuel for expiation, the perfect goal of neurosis is the assumption of all ailments. Neurosis and health go hand in hand.

As I say, every new arrival had to contract all the ailments of those present before he could begin to recover. It follows that it was in his interest to get infected as soon as possible. Group analysis was first of all a place and instrument for infection and epidemic; then perhaps it could also be a place and instrument for treatment and cure.

A speaking group exercises a huge fascination: it's a collective poet. There is a savage joy, panic and total, a prehistoric and animal joy in possessing oneself of a woman's dream. It's not like making love with her. It's much more. Making love—foreplay and penetration, caresses and ejaculation, orgasm—is all too banal by comparison. You don't know a person just because you live with her, eat with her, make love to her. You don't know her when you hear her confessions: dozens of confessors had listened to the men and women who came to Baart, but they hadn't known them the way Baart knew them. You only know people when you know their fantasies and dreams. That's where the depths of their hearts lie, in a place unknown even to themselves. Someone comes and says, "Who am I?", sits down with others, and together they seek an answer.

Here were both the marvelous and the disastrous sides of Baart's experiment. By sitting down and seeking together, in reality they were no longer trying to answer the question "Who am I?" but the question "Who are we?"

Early on, the I had to become we; then one examined who it was. Thus the initial question, the one that had brought each person there, could never again receive an answer. It was a little as though a traveler lost during a storm were to enter a cottage and ask, "How do I get to the city?", and the people inside were to reply, "To get to the woods, turn right." Baart's collective was a group of travelers that had strayed off the road to the city and was now content to find itself in the woods.

In the woods they had built a mini-city, a caricature of a city. It was not long before they began to make and sell T-shirts in the group with the professor's portrait on them, white T-shirts that could be worn either as underwear or instead of a shirt. The color of the professor's face was unnatural, dark brown rather than his customary pallor, but this was for technical reasons: you can't print pale gray on a white background. Even in his portrait the professor wore his very dark, almost black glasses. And he retained that tearful smile of his. It was from a photograph taken by a reporter, with a flash bulb. Every so often in fact reporters and curious members of the public came, as well as cameramen from the Italian State Radio and TV network or from commercial networks, who filmed the sessions, wrote notes, took

49

pictures, and even asked questions. Nothing betrayed their position as outsiders like their words. We were not disturbed by the hum of the TV cameras or the flash of the lights, these were instruments that had nothing to do with us, but their use of the word in that meeting room, within those walls, their use of words paralyzed and overwhelmed us like something sacrilegious. The word was not the vehicle, the sign of our illness: it was the illness. It was the "tongue" that was sick. It was as though a reporter, in writing an article on a clinic, were to stick his finger in a patient's open sore and ask the doctor, "What's this?" Thus the absurd, impossible, obtuse—in short, healthy—words of curious onlookers, journalists, and guests inflamed the group's already infected sores.

"Excuse me, professor," they would suddenly ask, "but the girl who spoke a little while ago, did she run away from home?"

Or: "Excuse me, professor, but who subsidizes these free sessions?"

As I made my way back to the station, to retrace in the opposite direction the seven hundred kilometers separating me from home, the reporters' questions kept tugging in my mind like dogs on a chain: why did the professor work gratis? was he rich? had those girls run away from home? where did they sleep? how did they live?

Questions with no answers are like an empty clothes rack: sooner or later you hang something there. One afternoon a fat brunette leaned over and whispered in the ear of another fat brunette sitting in front of me: "Fabio's not coming today, they've caught him." She didn't say, "He's been arrested," or "He's in jail," but "They've caught him." A person can land in jail for all sorts of reasons, but these days if he's caught, it means only one thing: he's planted a bomb. Tomorrow our descendants will have trouble understanding this very simple thing, which for us is elementary: we have a pile of dead bodies in our past and no idea how many murderers there may be, and so every month we add a few more. Each of us, ordinary people (who travel on business, eat in restaurants, go to the movies), have taken the same train, eaten in the same place, seen the same film, that a month before or a month later has figured or will figure in the indictment at some trial. In this climate, what does "They've caught Fabio" mean? Why did they catch him? Why was he here with us? What was his sickness?

Of course, these huge questions weren't even touched on in the group analysis. It was possible that among those hundred or so persons, someone with a crime to atone for might turn up for a day, a year, or three years, and speak with us, delve into us, listen to and judge our dreams and fantasies, without any of us knowing who he was. He was Fabio, just as others were Lidia, Giovanna, Marco; just as the professor was Baart. Gradually I realized that being part of that group meant losing one's individuality and becoming a ghost. The use of only first names or nicknames served precisely that function: separated from his or her identity, each became nobody. We might as well have been called by numbers. Our assembly was spontaneous but anonymous; deep and sincere but depersonalized; sentimental, erotic, and sexual but faceless, like the calls and encounters of ham radio operators who say to each other: "You have a lovely voice, K 82, and last night I dreamt I was making love to you." One night you get ready, at eleven-fifteen like every night, stick the antenna out the window and call K 82, you want to pursue your love affair with her. K 82 doesn't answer. For a while you go looking for her in the ether, your signals scour the ionosphere, but K 82 isn't there anymore. As compensation, there's WF 66. This WF 66 is new and enthusiastic, he follows you everywhere, yelling in your ears, "Do you hear me? Over," and you do hear him and will end by answering him. There's no more K 82, but no one is concerned: it wasn't she that the other ham radio operators were seeking, each was seeking someone but no one in particular.

Fabio had been caught, but the most important event in his life had no importance for us, and didn't even exist. He was one of a hundred, a hundredth of the group, but the group was still roughly a hundred, and so the group in analysis was intact and the same as before.

The effect of this discovery, that I was engaged in an analysis where whatever happened to me, including my own death, was of no importance, was to distance me irreversibly from the group. I could feel myself moving away by a sort of instinct for self-preservation. To me it didn't seem acceptable to live as though my death were negligible. Oddly enough, once I had made this discovery, I didn't immediately stop going to Rome, but on the contrary went more often than before. How come? Because the umbilical cord had not been broken, only nicked, and I hoped to break it as soon as possible. I stopped going to private sessions, and Baart immediately replaced me with someone else. I went only to the group sessions, where I began to feel more and more like an outsider, and to observe what was happening as though it no longer involved me. I even got to the point where I thought about going to the movies before and after the session with Baart; I would buy a Roman newspaper before leaving Padua and in the train calmly peruse the film listings for the capital, noting the times of the showings and checking on a map of Rome how far the movie theaters were from the Termini station and from Baart's headquarters, over there in the ghetto. I began to behave in ways unthinkable in analysis: I would arrive late, when the session had already begun; I would leave early, when it was barely underway. No one paid any attention, I hardly did myself.

Once I came in just in time to witness a serious and disturbing scene that ought to have aroused the group to rebellion. I come in, and a guy is talking. I can't see him, he's buried under a sea of heads. Windows closed, doors closed, sweaty air, smell of bodies. The guy has a squeaky little voice, you can tell he's excited, most likely it's the first time he's spoken, he keeps getting mixed up, he's concealing something, probably he means something else, from his voice you'd say he's a homosexual, and at that moment I sense that everybody is wondering: Is he gay? He senses it too, and cuts short his speech.

"Yes," he says with decision, "I'm gay."

"Get out."

Baart's order takes everyone by surprise. There's a moment of panic. No one understands what's happening, who should get out, or why. Baart's hand, forefinger extended, points to the door. His smile has vanished, his mouth is not trembling, his dark glasses prevent us from seeing his eyes, from seeing which way he's looking. The boy with the high-pitched voice is perhaps gathering up his things, perhaps leaving, no one can see him, he can't be very tall. The door opens and closes. He's gone. Someone from another quarantine, carrier of a germ different from ours, had entered our cabins and been kicked out.

The professor's mouth slackens, again his lips waver between smiling and grief, he bends the arm that had been extended toward the door and rests his hand on the desk. It's all over, we can resume.

The episode does not upset me, now nothing can reconcile me to this analysis and this group. I feel the need to get back to the station, and there I feel the need to go downstairs to the public baths and take a shower. While the scorching water flows over my body, hits my shoulders, runs down my loins and pubis, I realize that the shower is simply a way to wash the Roman experiment out of my system, make it flow away, cleanse myself. I shampoo my hair. I get out my razor and shave.

8. Insomnia on trains

I don't suppose anyone can understand what it's like to go from Padua to Rome more than once a week, month after month, without ever staying in a hotel. It doesn't cost much money since you can travel second class, the berth comes to about three thousand lire, you can carry your own food and drink if you like, and in Rome you can take buses if you're not in a hurry. But in terms of fatigue, sleep, and stress, the cost is unbearable and can take you over the edge of exhaustion. Many nights, on the return trip, shut up with five other persons in a compartment smaller than a solitary-confinement cell, with lights going on and off, having traveled uncomfortably on the way down the night before without a wink of sleep, having eaten badly, done three hours of analysis, one private and two with the group, and walked for hours and hours, I was afraid I'd be unable to cope a minute longer, and I'd repeat to myself like a litany *collābor-labĕris, collapsus sum, collābi*. Once the first person of the present indicative had filtered into my head through the crack of fatigue, it released the phobic-obsessive mechanism of perfectionism, and I had to run through the whole paradigm: *collābor-labĕris, collapsus sum, collābi*. There was no way I could shake off this conditioning. I could laugh at it but not deny it. I could debase it but not ignore it. And so I mangled the accents: *collăbor-labĕris, collapsus sum, collăbi*. I liked it better

55

that way. I ran through the paradigm like an intermittent burst of gunfire, *collăbor, collabĕris // collapsus sum, collăbi*, squeezing the trigger twice to keep time with the wheels of the train, which pounded the rails in a double refrain: *tata-tatum // tata-tatum*. The train and I formed a single crazy tangle, as beating the drum and reciting paradigms we sped northward for eight hours in the darkness of the night.

Between Rome and Florence, i.e., between 11:25 p.m. and 2 a.m., there was no letup. Sleep was in every minute portion of my body, in my stiff fingers, my heavy eyelids, which felt weighted down, my puffy lips, which felt swollen, my numb feet, which felt like someone else's. Everything in me slept, but I was awake. I wanted to sleep, but the will is not the only power in us that wants something. I doubt that in all those months I slept more than an occasional quarter of an hour on the trains. At the approaches to stations, I would go out in the corridor, moving on legs that weren't mine, open the window with hands that didn't feel like mine, and look out—Florence, Prato, Bologna, Ferrara. Each city was a heap of dark and solid houses, sleeping a soulless sleep. The automobiles that could be glimpsed driving with headlights on in the poorly lighted streets passed silently, without sounding their horns or braking, turned without showing taillights, and left the impression that their drivers were asleep too. Even the conductor in my car, between Rome and Florence, between Florence and Bologna, slept. Sitting on the folding seat at the end of the corridor, with his legs extended forward to keep himself from falling, his back against the corner of the car, his cap tipped over his eyes, his hands on his stomach with his fingers laced, his mouth open, he slept. I would watch him for half an hour at a time, thinking: If I could open my mouth like that, the swelling in my lips would go down; if I could stretch my legs like that, they'd be mine again; if I could lace my fingers like that, they'd loosen up; if I could tip a cap over my eyelids like that, they'd feel lighter. All of which meant: If I could become him, I'd sleep like him. I felt it was my single and greatest desire. In reality, as I learned later in my real analysis, I didn't cherish that wish at all, I didn't want to change in the slightest, everything in me aimed proudly at remaining what it was.

The most desperate nights on trains were those when it rained. On the train you don't hear the sound of the rain, one of the sweetest sounds in life. All of a sudden you see a sprinkling of drops on the window, and you don't know why. Then the drops multiply, run together, become rivulets, and they don't let up. The wind drives them backwards or up: raindrops on the window never descend. You observe the rain as though you were watching a silent film: a swirling phenomenon, which disrupts the world, spreads over every inch of it, but evokes no sound. Only when the train stops in stations do you hear the patter of drops hitting metal, they streak in all directions, like insects looking for a hole to get in. There's no hole, inside one is safe. Everybody's asleep, except you. You go out in the corridor for the fortieth time, you have the fortieth attack of colitis with diarrhea, that's why you couldn't sleep, you go in the toilet, but not in the first one where there's no more water, you've used it all up, you go in the second one, and sit yourself on the toilet bowl. You knew that on trains the rain doesn't go down but up. From the toilet bowl rises a blast of clammy air, besides it's now winter, the air brings with it a spray of drops that co-agulate on your skin, in the crack of your backside. Which goes rigid. But I must stop speaking like this, as though here there were some taboo. So let's say it: from the depths of the toilet bowl rises a vortex of cold air with a sprinkling of drops that coagulate around your sphincter. The sphincter closes, hermetically. The longer you stay, the worse it gets. You couldn't feel your hands, you couldn't feel your legs; now there's another part you can't feel: your ass. The pangs in your stomach twist and churn beneath your navel, and like kittens in a sack will never again find a way out. Come on, go back to bed. You've flushed but it wasn't necessary. It's a reflex.

You go back to bed. You no longer see the stations. You can't even calculate them by counting the stops, because when it rains the train always accumulates de-lays, and the delays cause more delays; it encounters a stop signal and sits there stalled for still longer; they forget that it's there on the tracks and give it the go-ahead only when they discover it's still there. So you learn to measure the journey by your watch: it's 2:25 a.m. and we've stopped for the fifth time, we're in Flo-rence, we should have got there at three minutes to two but we stopped four times, maybe there was a landslide on the tracks. Nobody talks when it rains at night. The few passengers who get on undress in the toilet, com-plain because there's no water, come out in gym suits and carrying their suitcases, check above the doors of the compartments for the number of their berth, here it is, they open the door with a bang, then close it softly, they've gone. You're alone again. Everyone's asleep except you.

At 4:05 the corridor becomes lively, the women are the first to emerge, grotesque with bathing caps, hairnets, or scarves on their heads, encased in jeans and loose blouses or baggy sweaters, with traces of yesterday's makeup still on their faces and the kit for today's makeup in their hands. They are impolite, bump into you, go by with lowered heads, they hate you for witnessing the temporary wreckage of their beauty, they make a dash for the toilet and lock themselves in with hysterical speed.

They open the door again immediately: there's no water, they have to find another toilet. As they come out, they give you a furious glance: how did they guess that you're the one who's used up all the water? This one here, plump and whitish, you've seen her before, two weeks ago, same time, same train. She will have seen you too. She will have gone to the toilet and found it dry, and coming out will have met your gaze. Ah yes, I'm the emptier of toilets. I go to the toilet sixty times a night, for nothing. It makes me mad that you go there for something.

We must be close to Bologna, the coming and going increases, now the corridor is more or less crowded, there's always someone going back or forth with a towel on his shoulder. The first suitcases emerge from the compartments, the passengers retrieve their documents from the conductor and get ready to disembark. They yawn, rub their eyes, and smile, glad to be in the world and to be what they are. There's no greater fortune than to be alive on this earth, to look at oneself in the mirror and say, "I'm happy." It's a good fortune I've never known, and which I don't even succeed in imagining. I always have the feeling that if someone says, "I'm glad to be alive," there must be a mistake, in him or me. One day I'll correct this mistake. I get off the train in advance, at any stop, and curl up on the tracks, in front of a wheel. The train starts and I stay there, besides I may be sleeping, and anyway I don't have the strength to get up. I'm sure that as soon as it starts they'll stop it, and everyone will wake up and get off. We're even, finally. Now there's something I could do.

The break in my relations with Baart put a stop to this idea too.

9. Star wars

Between one analysis and another there was always an interval of months. I tried to get along as best I could, but I only got sicker. It was like being buried in quicksand up to the thighs: you attempt to extricate yourself, strain now with one leg, now with the other, try to lift your knees, and the result is that you sink more rapidly still. The only remedy lies in outside help. Tarzan climbed to the top of a palm tree, bent it down in an arc to the quicksand, and when the explorer, who was about to be submerged, had grabbed hold of it with both hands, Tarzan retreated, walking backward along the trunk like a cat: thus relieved of his weight, the palm tree slowly straightened up, lifting the explorer into the air like a fish on a hook. Analysis is that palm tree.

For a certain period I followed on the heels of an analyst from Milan, who traveled throughout Italy and the world, analyzing his patients while standing in airports, or sitting in restaurants, or in taxis between the railroad station and the cathedral square. He worked with lightning speed, and always had an interpretation in advance; for him man was a creature who in infancy knew two languages but now spoke only one, and had therefore lost half of himself. Those who have remained whole (children, poets, lunatics) seem like geniuses or monsters. His method consisted in translating what the patient told him from one language to the other, so that

61

each half of the patient would know everything that the other half knew, he would go back to being whole, and become a child, poet, or lunatic again. To perform this task, he did what one customarily does in translations: he simply used the dictionary. You said something and he would translate or explain a few words. If, for example, I said, "Excuse me for being late," he translated: "Every excuse is always an accusation." The translation was not wrong, because if instead of giving me an appointment at the Linate airport, he'd given me one in the Piazza del Duomo or at the central station, I would have arrived on time. It was therefore as though I'd said to him: "It's your fault that I'm late."

Once I tried to engage him in a discussion that he wouldn't be able to get out of with a single remark. I wanted to argue. "Yesterday I saw a Bergman film, *The Seventh Seal*," I began. "It's a typical film about a mystical crisis." I waited for his reaction. His reaction was never what you expected. This time he replied, "There are too many *i*'s in that sentence," and I had the impression that the superabundance of *i*'s made it hard to translate into the other language. I thought of science-fiction films, in which the lost astronaut enters an urgent question in the computer, only to get the calm response: "Terminology unknown. Please reformulate."

This professor gave a great number of lectures, and invited me to all of them. Since our hours never lasted more than fifteen to thirty minutes, I had a real desire to get as much as I could out of the relationship, and therefore ran to listen to him whenever I could.

He charged admission, and so there was always a large audience, because if you paid for a ticket it was as though you were going to the theater. Had the lectures been free, probably no one would have come.

Expectations for his performance ran so high that the students printed phony tickets so as to be able to get in. But now he'd caught on to the trick, and the tickets you bought for his lectures were numbered and registered, and were carefully checked at the entrance to the auditorium. He organized several series of lectures in this way, and during that period private analysis was suspended, but we were all allowed to follow him as he moved about and to assimilate his words. Thus, once again, private analysis was contaminated by what he said in public. He became primarily a public figure, and since the lectures went on for a long time we all had the disagreeable impression that he preferred public moments to private ones. There was no encounter with the public that didn't end by becoming a spectacle. In this, the man showed an extraordinary ability, a primitive instinct that guided him infallibly, and helped him find the perfect word, gesture, pause, and reaction.

Arriving to speak in a municipal auditorium in Bologna, the professor found himself surrounded by about twenty young women, between twenty and thirty years old, who began a roundelay of dances and chants to prevent him from speaking. The subject was "The Violence of Feminism." The professor found himself isolated, unable to get out of the circle and ascend the platform to join his supporters. Some of his pupils, those who had been following him for years, took turns at the microphone, powerless, nervous, with flushed strained faces, trying to explain that the title of the lecture didn't mean that feminism is violent, for indeed the professor's thesis was that antifeminism and anti-Semitism were one and the same. In vain, for no one could hear them. They looked at the professor being thus held prisoner and suffered from it as from a desecration. The professor, impassive in his white suit, white shirt, and white necktie, stood smoking in the middle of the circle, which kept shouting and leaping like Indians around a stake.

The professor advanced slowly and sedately until he was close to the platform. The platform was surrounded. He started to sit down, but the chair was yanked out from under him, and he was again left standing. He smoked. He reached out to grasp the microphone, but the microphone was wrenched out from his hand; it rolled away on the floor and smashed. Smiling, he opened his mouth and pretended to speak. He was drowned out by a chorus of howls. The spectators in the hall protested, they had paid and wanted to hear. In their protests, they quarreled among themselves, since some insisted that the subject of the lecture was a provocation. The professor moved along the perimeter of the auditorium, where there was an aisle between the rows of seats and the wall. The troop of feminists, tasting victory since they had now driven him from the platform, followed him everywhere, to carry out what in military parlance is known as a mopping-up operation. Thus surrounded, he made the circuit of the hall, smiling and pointing with his hand now to one, now another, of the female hotheads who were insulting him. Some of his following of patients, especially the women, were in tears, watching him voluntarily endure this calvary, just as the apostles had watched Christ ascend Golgotha. Having gone all around the hall and now reached the door, the professor stopped and turned toward the audience, took a bow, stood upright again amid a burst of applause, and turning to right and left, indicated with a circular gesture of his hand the women who surrounded him, directing to them the applause that was drowning out the din, exactly like a band leader acknowledging the chorus girls at the end of the grand finale, bowed once more, turned around, opened the door, and left.

His pupils ran after him. While a feminist leaped onto the platform to improvise a justification for what had occurred, and scuffles broke out in the hall, the professor was on his way down the stairs, his cigar in his mouth.

"Where can I give the lecture?" he asked.

Rapid consultation. By now it was eleven o'clock at night. There was only the student center, which had been occupied for a week. We arrive at the student center, where there's a red flag at the entrance and a small group standing guard. After a brief discussion, they accept. We go in. Wall posters everywhere: raised fists, red flags, sickles, machine guns. It looks like a museum. Every room has a name, like the lecture halls at the University. We go in the Renato Curcio Hall.

The professor gets up on the platform, where he remains standing. He takes off his glasses, breathes on the lenses, wipes them with his handkerchief. We sit down, there are about a dozen of us. A girl prints a sign explaining the subject of the lecture, and pastes it on the door. The small room fills up.

The professor speaks of the crisis in the USSR, he begins by saying that Marx was not a Marxist. Two students ask him to repeat. He proceeds unperturbed, standing upright, absorbed. He declares that Marx is another Dante. Marxism is a straight line that runs from Marx to Hitler, this line is called conspiracy. We all stare at him with painful attention, to see how far he'll go: his skin is pale, his clothing white; calm and engrossed, he closes his eyes between sentences and smokes. All of a sudden his body gives off a shower of sparks, splinters of light, flashes. A dull rumble resounds in the room, then a rattle of explosions. Everybody flops on his belly, crawls under a chair, and lies there on the floor, out of sight. Like a star-wars hero, he looms out of that shower of light, motionless and invulnerable, bows his head slightly, and with the back of his hand brushes the drops of water from the lapel of his jacket. I look at him, from where I'm lying on the floor. The students have dropped a plastic bag full of water on the platform from above. He goes on to state that *Das Kapital* proclaims the apocalypse, meaning the descent from heaven to earth. That descent is the work of God. He has concluded, he steps down from the platform and crosses the room. From the floor the pupils look at him the way Patroclus looked at Hector, Hector at Achilles. Or the chicken the hawk. He's gone. Maybe he'll sleep in the city, maybe he'll take the train for Milan. It's 2:15 a.m. No one sees him off, he has no need of it, he's not like us. I never saw him again.

Besides, the doctor in Padua had put me on a two-year waiting list, and between the analysis in Venice, Rome, and Milan, the two years were coming to an end. Now finally I could go to him.

66

PART TWO

1. In the hospital

Thus it was that I began going to him four times a week. I would return home after the sessions as though empty and bled white. Arms limp, brain clogged. It's a miracle that in all those years I had at most only a couple of driving accidents. But after the session that I privately call the "session of the hanging breasts," I returned home with the sensation of having a different body, a freer brain. And I had a sudden inkling of what other people are like, those whose lives must normally be like this.

I lay down on the bed, trying to regain the position I generally assumed in analysis. But not curled up around the knot in my guts. Stretched out. Like a baby who's been copiously breast-fed. I felt sleepy all over. I fell asleep. That is to say, I took another step down from the stage I usually reached in my drowsy insomnia, when having arrived at the threshold of unconsciousness I would jump back and begin the descent all over again. This time I went beyond it, serenely. I woke up after an hour, feeling strong, but I lay still. Never had I felt so relaxed in every muscle. In all that tranquillity, I suddenly sensed danger.

I got up to sit on the edge of the bed, passing my hands over my forehead, my cheeks, my nose, as though checking them out. Everything in order. I get to my feet. My nose feels pleasantly warm, I like its warmth, today I really like myself. I hear a drop, a big drop, hit the floor, where it spatters into the shape of a ring. I live on the top floor—is the roof leaking? I look up, but the ceiling is white and dry, no holes. Another drop slides down and falls on the wooden floor. It's big and red. A big red drop of blood, a centimeter from the first. Another, two, three, four. Many. A pattern of red spots, like a burst of gunfire on a gangster's shirt. That's strange, blood is coming out of my nose. So far as I know, it's never happened to me before. I'll lose blood and make some more, I'll have new blood. I go in the bathroom, put a handkerchief under the cold water, and press it to my nose. The flow increases. I go back to the bed and stretch out. The blood drips into my throat, I swallow it in little gulps. I get up again, go to the refrigerator, take some ice, and hold it to my nose. I want to sneeze. I sneeze. The sneeze sprays blood everywhere, like splinters from a hand grenade. I go back to the washstand. The flow keeps pouring out. God damn it, I've broken a vein.

I'm alone in the house. I call a taxi, which comes immediately. I'm waiting for it in the street, pressing a handkerchief against my nose. "Hospital," I say in a nasal voice as I get in. The driver turns around. "Don't get blood on the upholstery," he orders me. I press the handkerchief still harder, and feel my eyes swell. I wouldn't be crying, would I? Are my nerves that shot? I rub my eyes with the back of my free hand, and the hand is covered with blood. Christ, the blood is coming out of my eyes! Is a whole cluster of veins broken? Am I bleeding to death? Is my skull full of blood?

The hospital is close by—here we are. The driver

jumps out immediately, opens the door for me, and yanks me out, he's afraid I'll mess his seat covers. He asks for three thousand lire. I take out my wallet but I don't succeed in opening it. He opens it for me before my eyes, takes out three thousand lire—he's honest. He puts the wallet back in my pocket and drives off. I head for Emergency, no one pays any attention to me. I tell the doorman that I'm losing a lot of blood, he's reading the *Corriere della Sera*, looks up from it, and points to a door, that's where I should go. I'm in a draught, I can tell I'm about to sneeze. I sneeze. The sneeze sprays drops everywhere, I think, like a hand grenade hurling splinters all around, but I only see the drops that get spattered on the white of the newspaper. The doorman sees them too, looks disgusted, puts away the newspaper, and presses a button. Two male nurses emerge from the door he had pointed out to me, they come toward me, maybe I ought to say something, but I'd rather explain with the facts, I remove the handkerchief from my nose and out comes a stream of blood all the way to the floor, like when you unscrew the nut under the crankcase to drain the oil. The nurses take a wheelchair and a sheet, an immense white sheet, and tell me to discharge the blood in it. They put me in an elevator, we go up to the third floor, on the third floor is the Otolaryngology ward, and just as you get to it there's a First Aid station, with two nurses and two doctors, one in a white jacket and one in a green jacket, like a surgeon. I wonder why. The one in the white jacket looks up my nostrils, and says that although he doesn't see anything, it's necessary to make a plug. They make a plug. It consists in blocking the nostrils with gauze, inserting a meter of gauze in each nostril, and pushing it in with a plastic screwdriver. The nose spreads out, it goes from one ear to the other. They close the opening of the nostrils with sticking plaster. It's nothing, I can go. They write me a prescription against infection, allergies, and itching. I call a taxi and go home. There's no one at home, my wife is out, my children are out, as always. They'll come back late, and sleep in their rooms. I have a temperature, I go to bed and fall asleep.

I wake up with a lump in my throat the size of a tennis ball. I sit up, with the wish to vomit; I vomit. Out comes a mass of blood, followed by filaments. I look at it. Old blood, black and dense, and fresh, red, liquid blood. I get to my feet; until it stops, it may be better not to stay lying down. By now I've lost two liters of blood, my legs won't hold me up, and yet I feel the impulse to experiment with this fatigue, to enjoy it (that's the right word), and as I totter along the hallway to the bathroom, I can no longer hide from myself the fact that I'm irresistibly happy. I'm sure that if I look at myself in the mirror, I'll see myself smiling. Nevertheless I really can't stand up, and when I sit down on the toilet I start staring at the door handle, wondering if I'll succeed in taking hold of it again. And besides it's now night. I go back to bed. Again I fall asleep.

I wake up with the feeling of having a snake in my throat: long and slimy, it moves partly in front of the tonsils, partly behind them. I have the wish to vomit. I vomit. It's a serpent of clotted blood, black and dense. Maybe it's better if I stay sitting up and awake, but by now I must have lost about two and a half liters of blood, I really can't stand up, and this is what gives me this sense of drunkenness that seems so close to euphoria. All I can do is sit there on the edge of the bed. I breathe rapidly, more rapidly than usual. My breathing is like a piston: I can feel it pulling a scratchy rope along the trachea, one millimeter at a time; millimeter by millimeter the rope reaches the threshold of the throat and hangs there. I have to vomit. I vomit. The usual bloody snake. I look at it, entranced. There's something in me bordering on bliss. I'm sick, finally, but really sick. Lord, I thank you. I'll stay awake and wait for dawn. Every two hours I vomit a little snake, depositing it delicately in a yellow plastic basin that I hold in front of me.

Around five o'clock, flooded by this inexplicable euphoria, I take an overall look at these little snakes, lined up alongside each another in the basin. Christ, there are so many. By now I must have lost three liters of blood, half of what I have in my body. If I wait any longer, I may not be able to make it. I awaken my wife, who grumbles a little, then goes to the telephone and calls an ambulance. They arrive in five minutes, come up to my floor; I'm waiting for them at the door. They want to pick me up bodily but I refuse, I like to feel my own weight, which I don't succeed in carrying, maybe I'll faint in the elevator, let's hope. In the elevator they press the wrong button because the elevator goes up instead of down, that's odd, because I'm on the top floor, and so if it goes up it'll soon break through the roof. The elevator stops with a jolt, we're on the ground floor, maybe they realized their mistake in mid-flight and reversed the direction. On the floor there's a stretcher waiting. I lie down on it, easing myself back, and at that moment, in a flash, I remember that this is the position of analysis, and I feel such a burst of happiness that I'm afraid I'll die of it. They carry me to the ambulance, and we speed away, while the city sleeps, its citizens so stupid and full of blood as to be forever unaware of this miracle at dawn. An occasional motorist, a few isolated pedestrians with their coat collars turned up, chilled and vindictive. Seeing them through the windows, I love them, I'm feeling so well. We're at the hospital. The doorman who was reading the *Corriere* is no longer there, he will have finished yesterday's newspaper and gone away, he'll come back when today's paper is ready. They take me up to the third floor in the elevator, there's only one nurse and one doctor. Just at that moment I have to vomit, I ask for a basin, and they give me a semicircular one. How am I supposed to deposit the snake in a semicircle? Usually they come out straight, but I try anyway. Nothing doing, the snake is straight. The doctor is disappointed, he looks at me irritably and tells me to lie down on the bed (so then they do analysis all over the place? they've finally realized that they should do analysis in First Aid stations? in ambulances?). He puts his tweezers in my right nostril, extracts the gauze, and deposits it in the basin; goes to my left nostril, extracts the gauze, and deposits it in the basin. Then he takes fresh gauze and with a plastic screwdriver rams it up my nose, first one nostril then the other. He closes it all with sticking plaster. Then he fills out a form admitting me to the hospital for tests. I'm assigned to the eighth floor, ward 17, bed 5.

Seventeen has always been my lucky number. The hospital is my habitat. I'm made for the hospital. My problem has been that the world isn't a hospital. I'd do well in a leper colony, like certain missionary friars. I know I resemble the friars, we used to travel to Rome together at night and split our cash. I mean, they took it from me, and then I got it back from the professor of the electric shocks. A nun is approaching along the corridor from the opposite direction, shortly we'll meet, she smiles at me. No friars here, but nuns, female friars that is, who immediately establish contact with me, stay up at night like me, look at me, and smile. We'll be friends, it looks like they've been expecting me for some time, ward 17 has ten beds, nine are occupied but one is empty and ready, the sheets are turned back waiting for me to slip into them, the stretcher comes to exactly the same level as the bed, together they form a single double bed, so that getting into the bed is like shifting to the other side. I'm all set.

So this is the hospital, where I belong. Nine patients, ten with me. Four or five are sleeping, five or four are watching me. They've watched me come in, scrutinized me while I shifted from stretcher to bed, and in that moment they checked arms and legs, stomach and back, to see if I have gauze on me, a bandage, and whether I'm bleeding. Nothing, all I have is this sticking plaster on my nose. So that's where my ailment is. What would it be? Why am I a patient? Will I be here for a week or a month? Will I die?

While I realize that these are their questions, I also realize what their answers must be. Lying there immobilized by a fatigue whose effects are the same as paralysis, they move only their eyes, and with their eyes they try to measure the conditions of others, and compare them to their own. The more advantageous the comparison, the greater their satisfaction. Their satisfaction is greatest if the one who appears before their eyes is fated to die that night. Because in reality—I actually had to enter a hospital at night to understand this, and this may be the reason I wanted to enter a hospital at night— the patient never wonders whether the other patient will die, but rather when. A healthy child thinks he's immortal. A healthy man thinks that death is remote and stationary. A patient is a patient because he has heard death take a step forward. And so he wonders: To whom has it come closest? to me? to you? to him? We're all condemned to death, but we're divided into two groups: those who have not received a warning and are healthy, and those who have received one and are sick. This warning is hanging in an aluminum frame at the foot of each patient's bed. It contains his fever chart, the time for his injections, the name of his medication, the record of the quantity of his urine and the frequency of his stool, and the date of his X-rays. Each of these entries gets multiplied by a coefficient, and the sum of the results means the life or death of the patient. This coefficient is secret. None of the patients knows it. Therefore all the calculations made by the patients are always haphazard and wrong, and inevitably give different results. Hence their confusion, and their mania for constantly spying on each other.

Now this particular situation in the hospital is the normal condition of life. Except that the games in life are disguised, by one's upbringing, manners, work, and passions. The hospital is the place where the mask is removed and we see ourselves naked. Misery, weakness, and shame are disclosed. One urinates in bed, into a receptacle. The urine is decanted into a measuring vial. It is held up to the light and examined, checked for color, clarity, turbidity, in the hope of finding the secret coefficient of the kidneys or of diabetes. Anyone who by tacit agreement has a higher coefficient of mortality immediately acquires privileges. They help him, they feed him. If he spills his urine on the sheets, they send for the nurses to change his bedding. If he goes to the toilet alone, they listen at the door to make sure he hasn't fallen on the floor, and hurry to help him if he has. But the patient who receives all these privileges, who feels that he's being constantly watched, and sees himself being served, pampered, escorted, guesses the reason, and becomes irascible, vindictive, intolerant, complaining.

I was 17/5. 17/7 had been admitted for angina pectoris, with violent contractions at the level of the sternum. With medication the contractions had disappeared. His breathing was normal, his color good. One day they come and tell him that he's being transferred to Surgery. He needs a heart valve. There are two doctors talking to him, and since you never see any of them, to see two at the same time gives rise to fear. Hospitals are like concentration camps, and the doctors are like the SS. In the concentration camps, there were very few SS, they were never seen, and to see more than one meant an impending execution.

The condemned man listened politely, almost gratefully. He was moved, two of them had come just for him. No sooner had the doctors left than his wife arrived. She came every morning. She was a woman of the lower middle class, cheap dress and purse, high heels, out of style. Until ten years ago they had belonged to the proletariat, and had seen the kitchen appliances, clothes, and bathrooms advertised on television as a goal. Now when they had finally succeeded in buying those clothes and shoes, the bourgeoisie had just given them up. This woman sits down on the bed and talks in a low voice to her husband. The husband doesn't answer. She has brought him a newspaper, which she puts in his hand; he throws it away without speaking. 17/3 gets out of bed, picks up the newspaper, lays it on 17/7's blankets, and returns to his place. Seeing the scene, the wife of 17/7 understands and asks, "What did the doctors tell you?"

17/4 suffered from diabetes and pleurisy. He was seventy years old. During the war he had been hit by a piece of shrapnel, had been operated on, and now he had a filter in his throat for breathing, similar to the carburator of an internal combustion engine. The filter was fine for inhaling and exhaling, but not for talking, because it didn't provide a sound box for the vocal cords. Thus in order to speak, he had to hold a wad of cotton over the filter, in such a way as to obstruct it at least partially. That way he could utter a few words, though actually he expressed himself with monosyllables, and by now had acquired a certain skill in choosing promptly, in the middle of a sentence that he couldn't pronounce in its entirety, the one brief word that was enough to condense its meaning. At night he slept with the wad of cotton within easy reach on the night stand. There were supposed to be only six beds in the ward, and the four additional ones had no lamp, bell, or wardrobe. The old man was assigned to one of these beds. To call the nurses, he had to ask 17/3 to ring the bell for him. All he had to do was turn toward 17/3, inhale as much air as he could, close the filter by pressing it with the cotton, and mutter, "You-ng ma-an!" 17/3 understood and rang the bell. The nurses came running.

One night, my second night, 17/4 reaches out his hand for the cotton and doesn't find it. He gropes, he rummages—nothing. It's a period when he needs insulin every night, he may be having one of these attacks. I haven't been there long enough to understand the hospital. I hear the old man's carburator gurgling like a flooded engine, and I assume it's normal. Of the others, those who are awake are concentrating on 17/7. He's the most serious case, the source of the greatest satisfaction, tomorrow they'll open his heart and insert an artificial valve. No one is even thinking about 17/4.

At 6:35, when the nurses arrive, 17/4 looks as though he's been painted, his face is purple and his arms blue. The nurses take him away quickly, attaching four casters to the four legs of the bed and running with the bed through the corridors. Consternation spreads in the room, as in a soccer stadium when there's been a sudden and accidental goal that no one has seen. Even 17/7 looks downcast: here was someone in a coma two meters away from his bed and he hadn't seen it, being completely absorbed by his own operation, which may not even happen today after all, but be put off until next week.

The hospital is not a place separated from the world, it is in the world and it is like the world. What happens inside the hospital (the others are glad when you're worse, because that's the only way that they can be better) is exactly what happens outside, but inside it's clearer and more complete. The fact is that I needed to enter this clarity, to withdraw for a while (for one or two weeks, but above all for a dozen nights) from the confusion that lies outside. But I also needed for my continually frustrated anxiety (the expectation of an illness that never comes) to be finally discharged in a concrete illness. And I needed for the pain in my nose—as though all the twinges had summoned a mass of blood—to be emptied in a long red cry of grief. I enjoyed it all: finally I was there, for three days I discharged a glassful of bloody tears every two hours, I now had "moderate metahemorraghic anemia," while around me one man was staring in terror at the ceiling because in a day or a week they would open his heart, and another had accumulated enough poison in his blood to become cyanotic, and no one had paid any attention to him. Well, that's life. I had looked for proof and I'd found it. I had wanted to expiate and I was expiating. I was in the right place and in the right frame of mind.

The hemorrhages began tapering off on the fifth day, when I had already received a first transfusion. My wife, who had come to see me on my first day in the hospital and had returned on the third (she had a lot to do, and meetings and committees consumed whatever free time she had left over from teaching school), showed up once more on the fifth, found me much better, and on her way out said she'd see me at home. It was precisely by the touch of her hands that I realized I was better: on the first and third days, they had felt to me as though they were on fire, as though she had a fever, and I didn't tell her so as not to frighten her. Now, on the fifth day, they felt warm, and as I became aware of this change, I realized that actually I was the one who had changed: she must have found my hands, on the first and third days, as cold as those of a corpse, and refrained from saying anything so as not to frighten me. Now she must have found them warm and realized that I was recovering, which is why she says she'll see me at home. I expect to go home in four or five days.

The notion of going home soon throws me into anxiety: I've hardly had time to suffer, they've only changed about half of my blood, expiation has hardly begun and it's already over. Now I may even succeed in sleeping at night.

In the hospital you have supper at six, at seven relatives come for a visit, at eight they go away, at nine the lights go out and you go to sleep. Now that I had a little blood in my veins and warm hands, I would get up at ten and go to the lavatory, sit on the toilet staring with resentment and humiliation at the handle of the door, which I would certainly be able to re-open with ease, go out, prowl along the corridor looking through open doors into the rooms of sufferers who were purifying themselves, the purest of all being those who slept with a family member watching over them, because they were dying, and thus purging their bodies of the last drop of guilt. When I got to the end of the corridor, I turned right and came out on a covered terrace.

I was on the eighth floor. From there you could see the whole city, with its lighted streets and squares: airport, railroad station, skyscrapers, factories, churches. Most lit up of all was the basilica of Sant'Antonio, which we call Il Santo. Tall, wide, with its swelling domes like

81

sails full of wind, and its pointed minarets like the masts of a sailing ship, it seemed to float above the city, bathed all over by yellowish floodlights. I spent entire nights on that terrace, without for a moment taking my eyes off Il Santo, just as when you go through a dark tunnel in a train and are unable to take your eyes off a lighted match.

The whole city slept, Il Santo shone, I had lost liters of blood and was finally where I belonged—in the hospital. Freed of all anxiety, I would have liked to sing.

2. Pain and penis

The hemorrhage caused a two-week interruption in the analysis. There were many reasons why I had brought on myself an uncontrollable hemorrhage and made them put me in the hospital—with such insistence that although my complaint would generally have been treated by an ear, nose, and throat doctor and not have required hospitalization, I had forced them to admit me to General Medicine. In analysis, as I may already have said, I learned that there are always many causes and explanations for every phenomenon. If a second cause explains a phenomenon, but has no connection with the first, it's valid just the same.

On returning to analysis and seeing the couch again, my first reaction was: What, did I leave it yesterday evening and come back this morning? Indeed, the position of the patient—always lying down, with permission to do anything, behave like a child, call out, dream aloud, cry, sigh—is the position of someone in analysis, and so I hadn't felt the two weeks of illness as a suspension of the analysis. On the contrary, they had seemed to me an uninterrupted analysis, twenty-four hours out of the twenty-four. You'll say: But the analyst wasn't there. I reply: But you never see the analyst, even when you're with him. Analysis creates for you the schizophrenic habit of talking to someone who's not there. The door to the room where the analysis took place was in a corner, and the couch in the opposite corner, so that from the couch I could never see either the analyst or the door, and often, as I've said—when I'd asked five, ten, twenty questions and received no answer to any of them—I was firmly convinced that the analyst had left. Getting up at the end of the hour, I would still find him in his place, but he could very well have just come back for the end of the session. To resolve this doubt, I had recourse to tricks, and asked questions that required an answer. For example: "What time is it?"

The silence that followed transformed my doubt into certainty: what would it cost him to say, "It's quarter of"? Would that be a departure from the script? If he didn't give some sort of answer, there could only be one reason: he wasn't there, he'd gone to the kitchen. I lay there listening and hearing through the walls footsteps in the distance, ever so faint, and indistinct words, muffled conversations.

So I had become used to talking by myself, as though he weren't there. If instead he was there, so much the better. If he moved a piece of paper, coughed, or struck a match, it meant he was there.

In short, this habit of feeling that I was alone even when I was in analysis drove me to feeling that I was in analysis even when I was in analysis . . . I mean when I was alone. And so I returned from the hospital and went back to analysis after half a month as though there hadn't been even an hour's break.

I immediately found everything the same as it was. Within fifteen minutes I'd picked up where we left off two weeks before.

I hadn't informed him that I was in the hospital, probably he didn't yet know about it, and I was in no hurry
to tell him, we had plenty of time for that. Everything
seemed logical to me and even foreseeable: I had put my
nose under the laser beam of his breast, and like a scalpel the laser had incised the sac of pus that had been
festering there for years. I had gone to have it drained,
a normal procedure. Never again would I have trouble
with my nose.

I needed to recover from all my other ailments. To
obtain this result, I had to discover two things: what his
other instruments of healing were, and what were my
other ailments.

The disappearance of one ailment had made all the
others take cover. Since they didn't want to be elimi-
nated, they stayed out of sight. Essentially I was all
right. My head, clear. My guts, untied. My ulcer, be-
having itself. My heart, at peace.

I might even have quit the analysis. I imagine that
under such circumstances analysis is frequently broken
off. This is the mistake made by General Custer: you see
a dust cloud in the distance and think the enemy is in
retreat. You advance victoriously and the enemy slaugh-
ters you. It's been an ambush.

In these cases, one must go forward with the suspicion that the enemy is everywhere, behind every bush.
In analysis, one must suspect that the silence of one's
ailments is the worst ailment of all.

I'd reached the point of begging my ailments to make
me ill, since I could no longer stand being well.

For a few sessions, we talked vaguely about the nose,
that fleshy projection that is hollow inside. I happened

to call it a "facial penis." I was proceeding by looking around and firing at random, like a paleface in an area infested with Apaches. The scout accompanying the paleface may happen to point to a clump of bushes and say:

"A hiding place."

The paleface, who had already gone ahead, turns back and fires. Inside there was an Apache. Behind me, my scout says softly:

"A facial penis?"

I was already thinking of something else, but I turned back and concentrated on the penis. The nose a facial penis? Why had I said that? Were the nasal hemorrhages my male menstruation, the cry of my man's uterus? What did the penis have to do with it? Instead of talking about its symbol, the nose, wasn't it better to talk about it directly?

So let's talk about it.

We started talking about it, and never stopped.

I had no idea it was so important. It was everything. It was a scepter. That was something I had learned as a child, only a few years old. It was after supper, getting close to bedtime, and I was standing on a table, wearing a nightshirt that came just to my groin, and waiting for my mother to put me to bed. Little boys and girls from various families were playing around me. A little girl my age looks up at me from below, sees my penis, and calls her mother.

"Look at him!" she complains. "Why don't I have one too?"

I was only a few years old, but my reaction was disproportionately triumphant, more or less as follows: I've fooled half the world. Now for the other half!

The pride of being male is multiplied from minute to minute, day to day, and year to year, but the final result of this operation indicates only a slight portion of the reality. For this river of pride had already been swelled by my father, and before him my grandfather, and before them all the males in our family, our village, and the world, and all these rivers of pride had emptied into me, filling me like a sea, even before I was born. I saw how people looked at pregnant women. If the belly is pointed, it's a boy. If it's flat, it's a girl. As though the fetus in the mother had an enormous penis, and this penis were erect and pressing against her navel. The pride of the male becomes the pride of the mother who gives birth to a male, and this pride begins when the mother realizes she has a pointed belly. If two pregnant women, one pointed and the other flat, meet while doing the shopping or drawing water at the well, the flat one looks in her humiliation at the pointed one as though imploring her: If you could only tell me how you managed it!

The male is a master, even if he doesn't want to be, because even if he doesn't act like a master, the women still behave like servants. He doesn't give orders, but they give them for him and obey. Ever since they were little girls, they've learned that the only purpose of their existence is to please the males, and lucky is she who pleases them all.

Thus the male learns that the purpose of his life is to have women, and lucky is he who has more than all the others.

I once saw a priest and a nun meet. The priest stood still and waited for her. The nun trotted up to him, made a bow, took his right hand and kissed it. I was a child, in kindergarten. The scene taught me that the separation between males and females holds true everywhere, even in the church, and life in the country, where one works with one's muscles, had taught me that this separation has its origins in physical strength: the man is stronger than the woman, that's all. This strength is connected with the penis. The bull is stronger than the ox. The man with an erection is stronger than the man with a limp penis. A sick man doesn't get an erection. Once he gets an erection, it means he's starting to recover. Erection and domination are synonyms. I wonder if the scepter was invented to resemble an erect penis.

But the fact that he carries this scepter brings with it endless liabilities. I've always seen the aged male propped up and assisted by his old wife. It's on the bodies of males that I've always seen paralysis of the limbs or face. Frequently there were men who after their fifties already walked with a cane. No women. When I saw a wheelchair, in all probability there was a man in it, almost never a woman. The same holds true even in the city, the only difference being that the wheelchair, instead of being wheeled manually, has an electric motor.

Paralysis, wheelchairs, canes, speech impediments, hardening of the arteries, a proneness to heart attacks: life seems always to be a war, and women aren't involved with war. The struggle for power is more exhausting than competition in giving pleasure.

What would that little girl, the one who wanted one like mine, have said if she had made the schizophrenic leap from excitation (everything is sex, I'm all sex) to depression (I've lost everything, I'm nothing anymore), several times a week, from month to month, year to year? If you keep bending and straightening an iron wire at the same point, it breaks. Excitation and depression equally unacknowledgable, equally irrepressible for everyone, and condemned by everyone. Every male breaks. Nothing of what the male says or does in the area of sex is normal or correct or wise. Everything is distorted, violent, contradictory. The sexual education of the male consists in abandoning the boy, amid silence, condemnation, and distortion, to invent by himself, over the years, whatever twists and contradictions best suit him and with which he can survive. To be a woman is difficult, and all of them complain that they can't cope. To be a male is impossible, and not one of them copes.

If a cut gets infected, if a finger is swollen, the little girl is allowed to cry, but not the little boy. If it's a question of going to the dispensary, of having a tooth pulled, the little girl is accompanied, the little boy is sent by himself, he's a man. If it's a question of going out in the dark, the girl can't, the boy must. The little girl is still her father's daughter at the age of sixty; at fifteen, the little boy is already his mother's older brother. For the woman, pain is a discourtesy; for the man, a test.

When I was a child, I had an abscess on my left leg, an abscess as big as a melon. I was operated on at home by a local doctor, without anaesthesia, sitting in a chair and with my father holding me from behind. This abscess was like a cavern full of pus. The doctor had made a hole at the top, like the chimney of a little house, and through the hole he lowered meters of sterilized gauze, which he then drew out with a gleaming tweezers, and thus he cleaned the cavern the way a chimney sweep cleans a chimney with his bundles of twigs. To me it felt as though they were burning my leg, and I couldn't understand why my father was on their side, against me. Pinned down on the chair, with the doctor kneeling in front of me and probing inside my abscess, and my father holding me fast from behind with his huge arms, I screamed for five minutes, sobbed for a quarter of an hour, and shivered for half an hour in a sweat. When the operation was over, the straw seat of the chair was soaking wet, but the sweat was warm and evaporated. My father put me on his bicycle and took me for a ride through the countryside to distract me and calm me down. As he pedaled, he leaned forward to whisper repeatedly in my ear, "Don't cry, you're a man."

We rode for hours. When I had calmed down a little, he took me home, carried me up the stairs in his arms, and put me to bed. Exhausted, shivering with fever, between waking and sleep, I pulled down my underpants and looked at that little thingamajig. Was that my consolation? But what could it ever give me to make up for so much pain? I knew it was supposed to be a good thing to have. And if I had said, "All that pain to have this penis," it would have been like saying, "All that pain to have this good thing," but with this difference: for me a penis was something that cost a lot of pain, and for everyone else it was just something good. I was four or five years old. From then on I was left with the unconscious feeling that pain and penis were inextricably bound together.

It was hard for me to pursue the path of these memories. They upset and humiliated me. Whenever I evoked some particularly painful one—for example, boys in elementary school comparing the length of their penises in order to establish a hierarchy of virility and hence of authority—I stopped and stalled for time, expecting the analyst to give me an award for the victory I'd won over my shame and forgetfulness. An appreciation, a compliment. He would lean forward and murmur, "Go on."

It was like pulling a marathon runner to his feet after he had collapsed at the finish line, and telling him to repeat the race.

We measured ourselves with rods and sticks, marked the respective lengths, and compared the results. There were some who tried to win by stretching it, you had to keep close watch to be sure that no one cheated. Every measurement took place before the eyes of everyone else. That's all.

"Go on."

What do you mean, run the marathon once more? There was a play-off among the top two or three, those with the biggest ones. As at the Olympics, there was a pause before the play-off. It would confer an important title for the rest of one's life. It was Mario who always won, everyone suspected he cheated, but no one could say how. Mario was the oldest, a chronic repeater in school, and his thing was straight. So when he got a hard-on, it was longer. Mario was a stocky kid, always eating, healthy and stupid. He'd certainly never had an abscess, and so his penis was a gift. I had paid for mine with blood and fever, and yet it was undeniably smaller. I never competed in the play-offs, I didn't get past the semifinals. That's all, I've finished.

"All right."

That was the formula with which every session ended. When he said, "All right," I was allowed to get up and leave. Which is what I did this time too.

There was a moment, at the end of the hallway, when he would pass in front of me to open the door and let me out. This was to happen this time too. As soon as I heard him approaching from behind, I said to myself with decision: Go on!

Since I had stopped to put on my overcoat, he caught up with me and passed me. He grasped the door handle and turned it. The door opened. He turned toward me, waiting for me to leave. For a split second, I took advantage of the movements that I had to make to put on my overcoat, bowed my head, and did something I had wanted to do for so many sessions, something I could no longer postpone: I stole a rapid glance in the direction of his penis, trying to guess what it looked like, how big it was.

That was how I saw what I hadn't noticed before. He wore his trousers low in the crotch, with plenty of space therefore reserved for his penis, which could expand there as in a basket. It could only be very big, very long. Certainly more so than mine.

You have to be a good sport about losing. As always, we shook hands in the doorway, and I said, "*Arrivederci*." He was supposed to reply "*Arrivederci*," as always, while imparting to me, by the firmness of his handshake

THE SICKNESS CALLED MAN

and the tone of his voice, such strength as I might need until our next meeting. Instead he too had a parting shot up his sleeve, and he sprang it on me by smiling slightly and murmuring, "All right," as though the session had only ended then and there with my glance at his penis.

He'd noticed it. Or rather, he'd expected it. All right, so much the better.

3. The spinal column

One of his potent therapeutic means had been the "hanging breasts." The "expanding penis" soon turned out to be another. I must bring myself to speak of this, if I want to tell the whole truth. Which is not only my whole truth, but yours as well. Anyone who has ears to listen should understand.

I suffered from back pain. This pain would strike suddenly, cut off my breathing, and make me go as stiff as though I were in a corset. One evening a woman friend telephones to ask if I'd like to go to the movies with her. I was alone, my wife was at a women's meeting, my older son at a political rally, the younger one at a concert. I say yes. I get ready. I shave with my electric razor, which for years now has been working poorly and pinches me because there's not enough current, the power is down in the city because of the oil shortage. I brush my teeth, and use the toothbrush to rinse them. I take a mouthful of water and spit it out. To spit I lean over the washbasin. It's while I'm leaning over like this that a flash of pain starts from the base of the spinal column and runs up it like an electric shock, radiating out through the ribs. I feel devastated. I can only bend my knees, which have remained intact, until they touch the tiles. Kneeling, I spit out the last water into the washbasin and wait. I breathe cautiously, so as not to stretch my ribs. Something tells me that the spine

94

mustn't make the slightest movement, it's like an electric battery, touch it and it shoots off sparks. I take a breath. My strength is coming back. If I can only get to the bed! Maybe I can get to my feet while keeping my spine straight as a board. I try. I raise myself up from a kneeling position by pushing with my arms on the washstand. I'm standing up. No sparks, only a kind of warning, like the slight shock you get when you brush against an electric socket. I walk, holding myself rigid, arrive at the bed, get into it on my knees, and stretch out, still rigid. I won't move again. My friend will have to go to the movies by herself. I hear the front door open and people coming in. From their voices they all sound like women. Someone comes in the bedroom. It's my wife.

"We're having our meeting in the living room," she says. "Don't disturb us."

I tell her I feel awful, and ask her to bring me a hot-water bottle. She stands there in the doorway, looking at me thoughtfully for a moment—how pretty she is, seen like this from below she looks taller, she has a slender figure, and looks good in military-style clothes, jackets with epaulettes, for example—I see her blue-gray eyes become attentive. If I get sick, it means I'm leaving her and the family in the lurch. I can't let myself do that, after all I'm the breadwinner in this house, the one with the penis. I feel guilty. I tell her it's nothing, it will soon pass. She goes out and prepares the hot-water bottle for me, first excusing herself with the other women, perhaps making some jesting remark about me, because I hear them laugh.

This back pain is always lying in ambush. It's as

though a mysterious but powerful force were following me around, to catch me by surprise when I'm about to go out, go to the movies, get out of bed, or take a walk, and brings me to my knees. By now it no longer scares me, since I've noticed that as soon as I fall on my knees, this threat abandons me, with a little caution I can get up, wait a while, and go on living. But the suddenness and violence of the attack makes it inevitable that part of my brain is always conscious of the spine, and this means I live in a state of apprehension. And inside me there is the conviction that the spine is one of the weak points in my orgasm . . . I mean my organism. It's rotten, or infected, or inflamed. It doesn't support me on my feet, it doesn't hold me up, it can't stand upright in a healthy way. It's disabled, it doesn't move.

My "disabled back" came to mind as soon as I noted his "expanding penis." They are two opposites. The former brings me to my knees, the latter stands up. The former is rigid, the latter elastic.

I had made a discovery, after the first year of analysis (in the first year I discovered nothing, indeed I became so idiotic as to lose the most elementary knowledge and was paralyzed by the simplest practical questions: do I have to fill out an application to get a telephone? since my salary is taxed at the source, do I have to pay taxes? I went to the Tax Bureau and explained my problem; they got suspicious and started investigating me). The discovery was this: between the moment you understand a symptom and the time it disappears there can be an interval of months or years. I'd dubbed this discovery the "pin effect," because it seemed to me it was like puncturing a balloon with a pin: you have to wait for it to deflate, and there's no law that says it has to deflate completely. The name "pin effect" and the image of the deflating balloon are explained by the fact that one of my most disturbing symptoms at the time was gas in the intestines. I swelled up to the point of bursting. No medicine did any good. The swelling constricted my heart and lungs. I discovered one, two, ten causes, but the symptom continued. It was like puncturing a hot-air balloon with one, two, ten pins: it doesn't even know it's been punctured, but in a month or a year it will be flat as a pancake.

Now the discovery of the two opposites, my "disabled back" and his "expanding penis," had the same kind of therapeutic effect: slow but irreversible.

I'd get up in the morning, saying to myself: Careful of the back. I'd move legs, arms, neck, but all my attention was concentrated on my spine, where the shock could begin without warning, and the muscles of my thorax were ready to block the lungs at the first stab of pain, to keep them from dilating and pressing against the ribs, making them crackle with pain.

The electric shock once caught me while I was in the men's room of a restaurant. My wife had gone to Venice, where Dacia Maraini was giving a talk on abortion; my younger son was visiting his grandparents, and the elder one was at a play by Dario Fo. I had felt depressed at the idea of eating alone again, and had gone to the restaurant if only to have a little company.

It was summer, and the restaurant was full of German tourists. First I went to the men's room. All the stalls are occupied, except one. I go in. I sit down. As I sit down, with my back hunched over, the stab of pain goes through me like a knife, cuts off my breathing, and leaves me drained of strength. A good thing I'm sitting down. I wait, something will happen. And while I'm sitting there rigid, I see a hand come creeping under the door and crawl along the floor toward my shoes. It advances slowly, sounding out the terrain. I'd like to stamp on it, but if I were to lift my foot, the knife would only sink deeper in the wound. I sit still, I can only move my eyes. The hand has its palm downward, and as it advances it sweeps the tiles. I feel sick and doubt that what I'm seeing is real. I've never before been locked in a toilet in the company of somebody else's hand. The hand is on my shoes, it feels them, climbs upward, turns aside, moves around them. God, let me stamp on it! If only I could raise my foot ten centimeters and slam it down, crushing the fingers, grinding my heel as on a cigarette butt! I'm sweating, I want to cry, it's absolutely incredible that someone is sticking his hand under the door of a toilet booth to sweep the tile floor with his fingertips: it makes no sense, has everyone in the world gone crazy? It's found something. The fingers close around a little piece of metal, a tiny black screw, perhaps a piece from a camera. It withdraws, fist clenched. To pass under the door—between door and tiles there's a crack five centimeters high—the fist has to reopen. Now it's gone. My wife is in Venice, my younger son with his grandparents, the older one with Dario Fo, and the hand has departed. I'm truly alone. Immobilized on the toilet by that stab of pain, like an impaled Muslim. God, make it possible for me to get up, I can't stay in the toilet until tomorrow, the place closes at midnight. Now I'll get up. First I'll do a test. I'll move the big toe on my right foot. It moves, I don't feel any pain. The nerve commanding the big toe has run in its sheath through my body. I try with my left foot. Ditto. Maybe I can breathe a little more freely. I'll try, if I feel the pain I'll stop. I don't feel it. So maybe I can even stand up on my feet, it all depends on whether I can keep the spinal column rigid, to the millimeter. If I make a mistake, I'll fall on my knees on the toilet. I swear that if I fall on the floor and a hand feels my nose, I'll eat it. I put my right hand on my right knee, my left hand on my left knee, apply pressure on elbows and knees and stand up slowly, the way the samurai do. I'm on my feet. I go out. The restaurant is full of smoke, several tables are empty, by now it's late, but the few Germans who are left are making so much noise that the room seems full. They're laughing, and one of them turns toward me and raises a tankard of beer. If only I'd been able to crush his hand, eat one of his fingers! I'm not hungry, and go home.

That's why I immediately thought of my back when I woke up: my "disabled back." But the discovery of his "expanding penis" began to monopolize all my thoughts, to the point of becoming a full-time preoccupation. That penis was his strength, and therefore mine as well. That penis became erect, and my back was healed. As it became erect, it swelled, with veins that branched toward right and left. It took the place of my spinal column, and of my ribs. Thus reclaimed and supplied with blood, now fluid and elastic, my spinal column could no longer do me ill, it could not "technically" ache: it was my strong point. In the evening, lying in bed, I listened to my spine radiating heat to my whole orgasm . . . I mean my whole organism, like a column of fire. I fell asleep thinking, and saying, "I'm warm," or, "My spine is warm," or "Warm me, spine!" I dropped off to sleep as in a hot bath. In the morning all my muscles were supple and relaxed, I moved easily, with agility and grace. I was hungry. I felt like a boiler, and my spine was the heating element in my watery body. I gurgled.

Had I discovered earlier this boon that came from him, my nosebleed would have been arrested. All I would have had to do was call him and ask him to come to the hospital, where the doctors were unable to check my "repeated hemorrhages," and once he was there, say, "Touch me here on the nose with the tip of your penis," and it would have made my painful, plugged-up nose all well, warm, and pliant.

It was in those months that I made the discovery of heat. His house was warm. It was an isolated house, a villa: you approached it through a large garden, surrounded by a hedge of evergreens. The gate was always open, and once through the gate you took a narrow gravel driveway, just wide enough for an automobile. I would arrive in my car and park to the right of his house. There was a small space there, I could even make a U-turn and leave the front of the car pointed toward the road.

That's what all bandits, thieves, and kidnappers do. They keep their car ready for a quick getaway.

Patients coming for analysis did likewise. We never discussed this, except indirectly. I didn't steal, kidnap, or murder—so why this careful preparation for flight? Deep down I was convinced that I got out of the place as though it were a garbage dump: I came to deposit guilt and shame, which I unloaded for an hour, then fled. That's what cats do. There were, however, other reasons as well. The license plate, for example. A car has a large plate in the back and a small one in front: everyone preferred to expose the small plate so that it, and he, wouldn't be recognized. Ahead of me in the early days was a Renault from Venice, but not for long, it lasted five or six months and then disappeared. Probably couldn't hold out. Then its place was taken by a small, very modest Fiat from Trieste, which always parked on the left. I never saw anyone get in it, because if I found the car still there when I arrived, which meant that whoever preceded me was still in the session, I skidded to the right, made a U-turn, and parked next to the wall, half hidden, so as not to see the other car except when it left and had turned onto the straight stretch of gravel leading to the gate. The others treated me with the same courtesy. It's an instinct. If someone arrived before my session was over, he parked his car on the side opposite mine and remained at the wheel. If he was just beginning analysis, he turned up his coat collar. If he was somewhat further along with his sessions, he smoked. If he was at the end, he got out of his car and walked around.

I thought it was mutual respect that prevented us from feeling curiosity about each other. But I came to realize that the truth was precisely the opposite.

It was his custom, if a session had to be cancelled, to warn his patients a month in advance, in the hope of avoiding possible abandonment crises. But he couldn't always do so. One Thursday in November (I had a mid-afternoon hour), he couldn't receive anyone else after

101

me, and just as I had got back in my car, while the person who followed me in analysis had already rung the bell—a quick little ring—I heard him come and open the door but stand there talking in a low voice. Odd, this had never happened before. Usually he greeted his patients quietly and smilingly let them in. Not this time—he sends the person away. He closes the door. The other person gets back in the car. Starts the motor. Before me? Before me. But shouldn't that person wait for me to go, for me to have left? He doesn't wait. Here everything explodes, the rules have been broken. I start my motor too. As soon as we turn onto the driveway leading to the gate (it's November, the air is dense with fog), the driveway suddenly lights up. From inside the house he must have turned on the lamps leading to the road. I slow down, ashamed, I still don't know why, as though I were being followed by a closed-circuit TV camera. We're on the road, the car in front of me turns right. I should turn left, but without thinking I turn right. The other car speeds up. I speed up too. It stops for a red light. I slow down, and catch up with it. The driver doesn't turn to look at me, but I see long hair to the shoulders, too much of it to be anything but a woman.

So he has a woman patient, and this woman doesn't play by the rules, she rings the bell before I've left, argues in the doorway, leaves before me, lets me see her rear license plate, VI 343 . . . , I can't see the rest, she's from Vicenza, she drives off in the fog, here I explode, and set off in pursuit of her. We have to settle this matter. She turns right, I turn right. Left, I turn left. She steps on the gas, but she has a small car, she won't get away from me. Here's Vicenza, recognizable by the many lights you see high up when you arrive, as though a formation of airplanes had stopped in mid-air. They're the villas on the hills. She takes a street toward the center, speeds, I speed, yellow traffic light, she stops, what does she think she's doing? Why doesn't she turn? I'm looking at her and hear a bang. Her car lurches, and so does mine. I've bumped into her. Now she'll get out and demand damages. Good, now I'll see who it is who doesn't play by the rules. But what's she doing? Why doesn't she move? Why doesn't she turn around? Nothing. Green light, she drives off, her rear bumper is all bent, the chassis dented. She's gone. Good, this will teach her that we're not supposed to see each other, next time she'll wait her turn. Anyway I'm going home now, I'll take the car to the garage. I'm euphoric. Then a little sad. Then in despair, once I've persuaded myself that I'll have to tell him about it. I won't be able to talk about anything else. This is all I'll have to say to him. And besides, every time I try to hide something, whatever I say has to do with that something. Maybe my car has been less damaged than the other one, but then it's bigger and more expensive. I'd willingly exchange it for hers, if that would close the whole incident. I'd give her whatever she wants. (Once when I was in school, I got beaten up by Mario, the boy with the biggest penis. Crying, I threatened him, "I'm going to tell my father." He sneered. Later he came back with a little neck chain, rubbed it on my sweater to show me how it shone, and whispered, "It's gold. Take it. Don't tell your father.")

103

PART THREE

1. The telephone rings

When one problem arose, all the other problems arose with it. When one symptom sprouted again, it made all the others sprout at the same time. The symptoms were like burrows in my orgas . . . my organism, and through these burrows the Sickness passed from one organ to another, invisible as a mole.

Whenever some point in these burrows was about to be uncovered, the animal inside went wild and scurried frantically everywhere. All the ills exploded simultaneously, and anxiety reached the point of paroxysm. It's at such moments as this that people quit analysis.

I was very punctual, I left my house forty-five minutes before my session, arrived at the villa with five to ten minutes to spare, waited on the outskirts (a bar, a side road) for four to nine minutes, started again, turned onto the driveway in the courtyard, parked to the right, and waited for the patient ahead of me to come out. From that moment my hour began (in the beginning, when he opened the door, I'd ask him shyly, "Has my time come?," until he pointed out to me that this is what prisoners about to be executed say, and so I changed to: "Am I on time?"). It never happened that the other patient infringed much on my time: a minute, two at the most. Once, however—it was in autumn—I had to wait five or six minutes more. I felt as though I was being robbed, I looked at the clock on the dashboard of the car, and checked the time by my wristwatch. There could be no doubt, they were stealing one minute after another from me. After two minutes I was anxious, after five minutes I felt the animal reawaken in the den of my guts, scurry to the den of the heart, then descend to the pancreas and the stomach. The burrow was a tunnel joining the dens like subway stations. Finally he comes out. Head bowed, muffled up. I can't make out his face, he looks like a criminal who's just been arrested. He gets in his car and drives off. It's my turn.

The same thing happened in the days that followed. After three or four times, rather than diminishing, the delay increased to as much as ten to fifteen minutes. You can bet they've changed the schedule without even telling me. I get out of my car and ring the bell. He comes to the door. "Am I on time?" "Yes, but please wait here," and he takes me into a small room one meter by two, a solitary-confinement cell. (Some years ago I had a skin ailment, red blisters erupted all over me, one every fifteen or twenty centimeters; I go to a specialist; skin specialists are also specialists in venereal diseases; I ring the bell, a nurse comes to let me in, and takes me through a labyrinth of little rooms like this one, even smaller, like telephone booths; she opens one of them and ushers me inside, saying, "You're number 17"; these cubicles, open at the top, are separated only by vertical partitions, and you can hear that they're all occupied: there must be some twenty of us patients waiting, some leafing through newspapers, some smoking, some in company with a friend and speaking in low voices; every so often the nurse's voice passes over our heads and calls: "Twelve." Number 12 moves. Light footsteps. It's a woman. She closes the door softly. What does she have? Syphilis? She's gone, vanished.) I wait. The delay gets to be twenty minutes, twenty-five. The analyst comes back, says, "Please wait a little longer," and disappears. But what's happening? Who is it who's stealing my time? Is he more important than I? More interesting? Is his animal fiercer than mine? Thirty. The door of the consulting room opens, and I hear footsteps. Sighs. Maybe sobs. Yes. Maybe it's a woman. Even at the door she's crying. I hear the door handle turn. What can she have? Schizophrenia? The door closes, they didn't even say goodbye. She's gone, vanished. It's my turn. I get up. As I get up, the animal slips out of the upper station—the heart—and burrows past the ulcer, then the pancreas, then the intestines. It falls asleep, I don't feel it anymore. But yes, the patient before me was worse off than I, all chewed up inside, and had taken a little of my time in order to survive a few more days. Other people are sick too. I must stop bumping into them and counting minutes. So long as he kept me for the time agreed upon, forty-five minutes, I was satisfied.

While I lay there, saying nothing, and he perhaps (I don't know) was sitting behind me, I heard the telephone ring, far away, in some other room. It rang again. I begged silently: Don't go, stay with me.

The animal in my guts woke up, climbed back through the burrow. Another ring. (But who can it be? Don't they know I'm here? Don't desert me.)

Another ring and it stopped, someone had gone to answer. His wife, of course.

The animal went back down and disappeared.

I had nothing to say for the whole hour, but it was as though I were saying to him: Thank your wife for me.

Surely he'd understood, because I heard him tap his cigarette twice with his finger to knock off the ashes, as he did every time I confessed something that pained me. I wonder if his wife ever knew of my thanks.

It seemed to me that not only he but his whole family took part in my analysis, insofar as was possible, more than was possible.

It happened a few times that no one was home, and the phone rang for a long time in the middle of my sessions. After the fourth or fifth ring, I began to be afraid: Now he'll go and leave me alone. What will I do?

He didn't go, he stayed there motionless (assuming he wasn't in some other room). I'm still grateful to him for this, and when I think of the few times when some-one has shown affection for me, I remember those mo-ments.

(It's your wife, I'd think. Stay here.)

He'd sigh and puff. Another ring.

(It's your mother. Don't go.)

A smacking sound, like two lips parting. He's opened his mouth, shortly he'll speak, maybe tell me I must leave. He inhaled again. He tapped his cigarette with his forefinger. The ashes must surely have fallen, a little weightless residue. Silence. He sat there. The min-utes passed. The animal was standing on its feet in the den of my guts, uncertain whether to start climbing. The hour passed.

(Go to your mother.)

"All right."

*   *   *

I began to envy the woman who came before me, because she stayed a few minutes longer. I envied her for this, but since I knew that she stayed longer because she needed him more, meaning she was worse off than I, I envied her ailments and would have liked to take possession of them. I had an extraordinary ability to take possession of other people's ailments. Someone had only to say to me, "I suffer from extrasystole," and I, who had never had that complaint, would start thinking about it, investigating exactly what it was, and in three days would succeed in reproducing it in myself: I'd go to bed nights and hear my heart missing beats, then recovering with a stronger beat. If I was to go to sleep, I needed for the rhythm of my heart to be regular for a long stretch, but this no longer happened. I had a new ailment. I thought it was fatal: the heart pauses, now it's stopped; it's started up again with an effort, the next time it won't succeed; it's finished.

I mentioned it to him, and he said nothing. I went ahead with other problems, but my problem was that one. I came back to it, introducing it as a catastrophe; he became attentive, and so I explained the phenomenon again. He seemed irritated, and for the first time—leaning over me—reproached me in more or less these words:

"You announce terrible things, and then you come out with such—" he sought the right expression and found it—"small fry."

The term "small fry" struck me because of its double meaning: it indicates something of little importance, but also little fish, good only for serving with more substantial fried dishes. Something like the greenery for

111

bouquets of flowers. Now, in happy moments I imagined my body as a water boiler, and my spine as an electric heating element. The small-fry image made me feel as though I were made of water. I felt the heating element get red-hot, the body get warm; the heart was beating as powerfully as an internal combustion engine. The extrasystole vanished and didn't come back. After a week or two, I told him about it, and attributed the disappearance to his use of the term "small fry." If he'd used another term, the phenomenon would have taken another course, I don't know what, but instead it was immediately dissolved, because he had found a key word in my psychological mechanism. He thought about it and added:

"Yes, but you also made it disappear because I"—he sought the right words and found them—"wasn't interested."

At that moment I was holding my left arm extended off the couch, the fingers clenched in a fist. The moment in which he sought the right word always made me tighten up, like a coiled spring. When he said, "I wasn't interested," my left hand opened and the closed fingers relaxed, as when a spring is released. It was only after making this gesture that I became aware of it.

"I do that with my hand," I said, repeating the gesture, "as an exercise to loosen up the fingers."

"Yes," he replied, with a rapidity that astonished me—he had obviously noticed the gesture, and had his own interpretation ready—"but also to ward off my response."

It was true. That response had irritated me, like a humiliation. The things I suffered didn't interest him?

112

While he was so interested in the woman who preceded me that he prolonged her hour into mine? So what did she have that I didn't have?

(I had a little sister, and once when she was three years old she went running like mad and then came back to our father, saying, with a worried look, "Feel my heart."

Our father leaned his head, put his left ear on her heart, and straightening up, exclaimed cheerfully, "It's beating so fast!"

My little sister laughed with delight. Alone on the sidelines, I had watched the scene. I was five years old. I started running, first slowly, then faster and faster, and returning to my father I took his hand and placed it on my chest, saying, "Feel mine."

He pushed me away with his hand.)

Arriving on the couch after her—one minute after she had got up—I sought the precious . . . damn it, I meant the precise place where she had lain, sought with the forms of my body—buttocks, nape—the hollows left by the forms of her body so as to reoccupy and fill them. So as to be what she was. So as to have her ailments. So as to be interesting in his eyes. If I felt a little heat—the heat left by her skin—I concentrated on it entirely. If I smelled a little perfume—in the air, but mostly on the pillow—I breathed deeply.

Once, in the middle of winter, his heating system broke down, and he had placed on the couch a heavy woolen blanket. When I arrived, I found it bunched up at the foot of the couch, having just been thrown off by the previous patient. I took hold of it by a corner, lifted it up, lay down under it, and drew it over me, and as I arranged it on my body by pulling one edge over my chin, I sought with my nose and mouth the exact spot where it had lain on her chin and become imbued with her moist breath, her odor, her virus: if she had tuberculosis, I wanted to catch it too.

Other times, when the heat didn't work or there was no oil—which frequently happened in his village, since it was a small village on the hills, and the oil, what little there was, was monopolized by the city—he put on an electric heater. Arriving, I waited a moment at the door, in the cold, then crossed the small, cold vestibule, was admitted to the consulting room, and immediately felt wrapped in warmth. Looking around, I'd discover the electric heater hidden in a corner. As soon as I noticed it, I exclaimed to myself: He's done it for me!

For the whole hour the heater was there, red-hot. Every so often it made a click, as though calling attention to itself. The clicks of the metal, which increased as the temperature rose, came to play a supporting role in our conversation or our silence, to the point of becoming the essential element.

"I've had a dream, which I don't completely understand, and I'd like to tell you about it."

Click: Go ahead, it's warm in here, just for you.

I described the dream. A silence followed (a long silence always followed my telling of a dream; sometimes I told it in five minutes, after which neither of us spoke for the rest of the hour; it could happen, however, that in that silence the dream became clear in my mind and his. Silence is to communication as a darkroom is to photography: it's there that the photograph is developed). In the silence, came the clicks of the electric heater. I'd hear them and think: How nice to be silent in winter, listening to a heater that clicks. One could write a poem about it.

I like the fact that I never saw him write, never saw pen and paper on his desk, neither before nor after the session. It leads me to think that what there was between us has remained so, reserved entirely for the two of us, and not for others. It seems to me that if an analyst takes notes during the sessions, when the analysis is over he should summon the patient for a supplementary ceremony: the burning of the notes in the fireplace. Such are the hours spent in silence: hours in which one talks a lot but burns the notes during the session. The electric heater is like a fire, it crackles and snaps. Its heat is dry.

(When I was little, I had no gloves, and in winter my hands got terribly chapped; the little cracks were reddish purple, like the marks of a colored pencil; one evening when I had my hand on the table, palm downward, my mother noticed all those signs and scribbles. She said nothing, she never mentioned it, but I realized that her eyes were full of tears. For this reason I never wear gloves, even now when she's dead: so as to repeat that scene eternally. Whenever I go into big department stores and see endless counters with woolen and leather gloves, and customers choosing and buying, I always think: Their mothers don't love them. My sons have ski mittens made of goosedown: their hands are burning. My wife has suede gloves, a black pair, a white pair, a red pair. I have none.)

*   *   *

When the electric heater was in the room, and I had discovered where it was—sometimes it was on the right, in a corner; sometimes under the window, behind the curtain; sometimes on the left, in the space between the bookshelf and the wall—I turned my head and talked in its direction. I looked for it as soon as I came in, and glanced at it on my way out. Those who have been in the army will know what I mean. When you report to headquarters, the thing you have to salute, first upon entering and last when leaving, is the flag. Whenever in winter, setting out from my house in the car, I heard the motor having trouble getting started because of the cold, I'd think: Let's hope that his heat's not working. Because then he'd have to worry about me and my hands.

2. A stone, perhaps

His "expanding penis" had become my strength, it was mine. My own was no longer nothing. It began to get sick, but still no one paid it much attention. If a cocker spaniel sneezes, you take it to the vet, but you leave a stray dog where it is even if it has pneumonia.

It began to get sick, and the first thing was a swollen vein (or nerve, or gland) at the tip, on the left, under the foreskin, next to the groove at the top of the glans. I would wake up, and that nerve would be swollen and inflamed, as though there were a clot or an infection. By the end of the day it was smooth and normal. Next day, turgid and varicose. I began smearing it with penicillin ointment in the evening. Calmly, in the empty apartment, I'd apply this penicillin, with or without a wad of cotton rolled and wrapped around the glans like a little life jacket. The penicillin had no effect on the ailment for which I was using it: the ailment disappeared and came back whether I used the penicillin or not; it could be at its height after a copious application, and no longer there after a night without treatment. Since it didn't hurt, I stopped treating it.

Months went by. One Saturday, while taking a walk in the city, I feel a pain in my penis, or not so much a pain as a sensation. Bah, an irritation. I go into a pharmacy and buy Elmitol. I take two tablets. I keep strolling. Mine is a wonderful city, which is to say, it's been

117

inhabited by generations of people with interesting neuroses: Via San Francesco, the obsessive ritual of prayer (the arcades have little cupolas and apses like the naves of churches); Piazza della Frutta and Piazza delle Erbe, the psychosis of money (within a few square meters, banks, tribunal, markets, and prisons). I enjoy idling with my own neurosis in the age-old river of other people's neuroses.

All of a sudden, the penis makes itself felt a little more, indeed much more. It really hurts. I go into a bar. Men's room. In the back. A drop, but such pain as though it were a drop of blood. Something must be torn inside. Telephone, a token, I call my health insurance doctor, it's the time when he's available. He tells me that Elmitol isn't strong enough, I should immediately take Thyosulfil-A (he repeats: A), a double dose; then apply Uretal with a tube, before having my bladder checked. I buy this painkiller and swallow it. I had thought that the burrow went as far as the guts, not that it went down further still. The animal has certainly dug deep, and it's still scratching.

What time can it be? Eight o'clock. The pain increases, I'd better take shelter in some men's room or else I'll faint. In the men's room I really don't know what to do, since I don't succeed in urinating: one drop, which burns like a fuse as it passes. I can hardly breathe, the pain is so paralyzing. But how can such an insignificant penis hurt so much? I look at myself in the mirror: around my nose there are creases, which I've never had before, and my lips are full of vertical cracks as though broken up into segments. I go out, a hundred meters, another men's room: same cracks, same creases, same drop. What time can it be? 8:30. I arrive home. Another drop. I lie down on the bed, if there were someone around I'd ask for a blanket, but by myself I don't feel like looking for it. I curl up and wait. I really have to urinate. God, it will be a river of fire. If someone were here, I'd leave the door open and say, "Don't come in," but there's no one, I leave it open and say nothing. Here's the toilet, the most welcome of human inventions. They say there are bathrooms with the toilet hidden in an alcove: you go in and you don't see the toilet. If I didn't see it now, I'd faint. What time can it be? Nine o'clock. I don't have the strength to sit down, I lean with my hands against the wall, bend forward, open my fly. I'm ready. A drop starts from deep inside, rises to the surface, gets ready to come out: it goes forward like a drill, gouging as it goes. It will be blood-red. It comes out. It's red blood. It hangs for a moment at the tip, long enough for me to examine it. I do examine it. It falls, it's gone. It hurts so much and I feel so weak that my body trembles, quivering at the level of the pelvis like a cord stretched taut.

I look at my penis. "Why does he have one and I don't?" that five-year-old girl had asked her mother on seeing it. A third of a century has gone by. "You want it?" I answer her, "I'll exchange all of mine for half of yours."

I need Lispamin, there must be some in the refrigerator. The refrigerator is fifteen meters away, I can make it by myself. And anyway I am by myself, there's no point talking about it. Here I am at the refrigerator. It's 9:30. There's Lispamin, but only for children. I'd bought it for them. I insert two suppositories, to make an adult dose. I drag myself to the bed. It's a question of time. God, how sick I feel. If it should go on like this much longer, I'd have only this *idée fixe* and all the others would disappear. What time can it be? Ten o'clock. That's when my younger son is supposed to come home, he's gone to do his homework with his school friends, and have dinner with them. He'll be back soon. Meanwhile let's go in the bathroom, for one last try. I take up the same position as before. The drill starts up again, but the groove is already dug, it scrapes the walls a little, a red drop comes out, another one pink, then yellowish, golden. They don't burn. My body trembles, quivering at the level of the pelvis, but with a feeling of liberation that runs throughout it. I remove my hands from the wall, letting myself slide down, rotating from right to left, counterclockwise, and find myself sitting on the toilet, the most welcome of human inventions. It's over, now we can go on with the struggle. It must have been a kidney spasm or an inflammation of the urethra. By now it's too late, we'll find out tomorrow. So until tomorrow.

Next day I go to the University Polyclinic, the Urology section. They give me a ticket with the number 23. When number 23's turn comes, I go in. Inside, separated by partitions, are lots of little white cubicles. Each with a cot. I lie down on the cot, I'm in analysis, I explain my ailment. The doctor unzips my fly in one stroke, extracts my penis, inserts a tweezers, spreads it (ai-yai!), and penetrates it with a ray of light, like a laser. "I don't see anything," he says, turning his back as though finished. What do you mean, you don't see anything? The pain was enough to make you faint, I wouldn't be able to stand it a second time. The doctor has gone into the next cubicle, and now returns with another doctor.

"*Regardez, vous aussi,*" he says.

What, are we in France? The newcomer leans forward, gives me a glance. "*Vous permettez, monsieur.*" He inserts his tweezers and directs the laser.

I'm flabbergasted. He asks my permission and then looks up my urethra, while dilating it. First Italy, and now France is stooping over my penis. I'm lying on the table like a corpse. It's like an autopsy. He looks. He looks again. He stands up, stern.

"*Un petit caillou, peut-être.*"

A stone, perhaps. "*Ça peut se répéter?*" I ask the Frenchman.

"Maybe in a year, maybe in ten, maybe never," replies the Italian.

I sit up. "Could I die?" I ask the Italian.

"*Non,*" replies the Frenchman. "*C'est très douloureux, mais ce n'est pas grave.*"

They disappear into the next cubicle. I get up. I zip my pants, saying as I leave: "Let's go, little one."

3. The earthquake

I began to dream at a dizzying rate. I had two or three dreams a night, and would wake up at dawn more tired than when I went to bed. For the whole day I went around in a daze. Submerged in my underground, disorderly, and chaotic world, I no longer had any connection with the world of other people: an earthquake might happen and I wouldn't have cared. And in fact one did happen: one night when I was in the bathroom washing my hands, and I had the impression that the washbasin had jumped at me.

That's funny, I thought, the washbasin just jumped.

While I'm thinking this, the washbasin makes another jump back. I extend my hands to keep them under the faucet, and at that moment all the combs, hairpins, lipstick, and other tiny objects that my wife keeps on the shelf under the mirror slip and fall into the washbasin. I look at myself in the mirror and realize it's an earthquake. My first reaction was one of astonishment: I'd always thought that earthquakes made the floor tremble, and instead the only thing that wobbled here in my house was the vertical wall. I live on the fifth floor, and I imagined the whole building bending back and forth in the earthquake like a tree in the wind. I go down in the street, the street is full. I would never have thought the neighborhood had so many people. They're all looking for their family members, no family is complete, we're living in a time when the family is no more. I'm alone. Everyone has the same thought: that the house not collapse. I think of him, up there on the hills: will he have gone out? will he have got dressed? where will he sleep? will we see each other tomorrow?

Next day we do see each other, and resume talking about matters at hand. I had begun telling him about a dream, I go on with it. At a certain point I have the distinct impression that the couch is wobbling, and banging slightly against the wall. I'm not sure, it could be my body. A body in analysis sometimes flops around like this. I look at the time: 10:25. Next day, opening the newspaper, I discover that at 10:25 there had been a tremor. It makes no difference to me, what happens inside me is infinitely more dramatic. The world pursues its path and I pursue mine.

I haven't the slightest doubt that every man will condemn me for this, but I also haven't the slightest doubt that any man, suddenly finding himself in my shoes, would behave like me. At that moment I was in a phase where having brought him everything I could, I was beginning to take something back, and beginning to spy on and dream about his loves, his sex organ, his fantasies. I dreamt I penetrated deep into his house, no longer did I stop in the small consulting room, but proceeded through the hallways and reached his bathroom. His bathroom was surrounded by a low wall that didn't go all the way to the ceiling. On this wall perched a woman, and she was his woman: legs spread, knees wide apart, she displayed her wide-open vagina, its interior pulsing and engulfing like quicksand. Any man on earth, who for years had been bringing his memories, loves, dreams, fantasies, and sex organ to another man much stronger than himself, and who was now beginning to take something back, starting with the other man's woman—it would certainly take more than an earthquake to move him.

One dream followed another, creating a world so intricate that it was absolutely impossible to disentangle it all. We began with interpretations, which were like holes drilled to connect the underground world with the world on the surface. But after a few months this operation turned out to be dangerous and had to be abandoned: the surface to be dug (symbols, memories, individuals, situations, from early childhood to the present) needed such frequent and extensive drilling that had it been carried out, it would have made everything collapse. Already it had fallen at more than one point, and I can't always say whether some event that I'll never forget really happened or if I simply dreamt it. He must have thought this tumultuous dream activity was a form of resistance, a barrage of fire that I was deploying in front of him just as he was preparing to delve into me. He therefore adopted a tactic that at the time I found intolerable: he stopped interpreting, he didn't respond. He was waiting for the barrage to subside. As a result, it's only at the end that this underground passage emerges into the open air, while for most of its length the tunnel goes on in almost total darkness. Every so often, in order to hold out and keep going, it was necessary to insert a simple ventilation pipe. This happened especially when it came to nightmares. This means that when speaking of my dreams, I don't know what I'm saying, and am therefore wholly sincere. I don't think one can be sincere unless he's unaware of what he's saying. The man who says what he knows, or knows what he says, is lying.

4. The tunnel of dreams

My wife is ill, and construction work is going on in the hotel or rest home where we're staying. The doctor who was treating my wife has had a concussion: his head has been split open, and his brain has come out of the cranium. Now I must put the brain back in the skull. The doctor is in a coma. The brain is back in place, it's not that the cranium is deformed, but I don't know how to close the seams. If only I had some glue! My wife stands beside me, tapping the ground with the end of her umbrella, and all I can see is this skull that I'm unable to seal and this pointed umbrella tapping the ground beside me.

(Nowadays it's impossible to understand women: those who up until yesterday were still able to treat them today have burst their brains. And yet the woman imperiously demands to be taken care of: she is still the woman of yesterday, who needs to be taken care of, but she is also a new woman, who has power and exercises it. That pointed umbrella being tapped on the ground like a lance is the symbol of the power that has been seized by women. An anxiety-dream, with no solution.)

I was in the same room with Paul VI, I didn't look at him (he was behind me), and didn't say anything, because I wasn't sure he could understand me (he's a foreigner, from a country that begins with P, perhaps Patagonia), but I felt safe simply because he was there: it gave me a guarantee of eternal salvation.

126

(The power of the analyst is perceived as holy: his presence is enough to ensure salvation. It's not necessary to speak, and anyway speech is impossible: we are at the beginning of the analysis, and the analyst still doesn't speak my language.)

Danger lies at the top of the mountain. I'm holding fast with both hands to the slope, which is narrow, steep, and very high. I've almost arrived, but I don't quite dare ascend to the top, I cling there as though my hands were hooks. I don't dare let go. Airplanes go by. One comes near. I recognize it: it's a French Mirage. A minister has said that Mirages travel with the speed of a pistol shot. It has swept wings. The pilot idles the plane near me, and grazes me with its tail. But it's not a pilot, it's a pilotess, and the tail of the plane is a skirt, shaped like the exhaust of a jet. So many planes, so many pilotesses. I cling there like King Kong at the top of the Empire State Building. They graze me or fire at me. I'm terrified that the exhaust fumes will make me fall. One comes behind me, and with the nose of her plane jabs me in the back, which remains disabled, then flies around in front and strikes at my penis, which bleeds, then at my guts, which swell up, then at my heart, which develops extrasystole; these quick blows hurt and may make me fall, I'm about to fall, from a height of three thousand meters, down into a valley where all these pilotesses have landed and lined up in ranks, each one pointing to her own plane, where there's the inscription Mira-Miracle, as though whoever had written it stammered and didn't know French.

(This is a very detailed dream, like a short story. I imagine the scene in the film King Kong *where this giant ape holds the woman in his arms and looks at her tenderly, and her ordering*

him, "Put me down, you antifeminist monster." The dream shows on the one hand the situation of the male, who is in danger, about to fall or be hurled down, and on the other the condition of the woman, who travels securely in the most perfect of airplanes and gives vent to her sadism by firing, colliding, and jabbing. The blows are felt in the organs where anxiety is somaticized: penis, guts, heart. Not the nose, by now perhaps recovered from its bleeding. The choice of the Mirage jet as a vehicle of the woman is owing perhaps to the memory of a line in Dante about Beatrice, who "came / from heaven to earth as evidence of a miracle": this may be why the name Mirage turns into Miracle.)

We're on safari with a jeep, a strange sort of jeep with the driver's seat in the back. I'm sitting in front on the left and on the seat to my right is a leopard, stretched out under the window, or rather with its head out the window, which drops (like a guillotine) and slices its neck. It dies quietly. Every time that there's a crossing, the jeep turns to the left. I keep one hand on the leopard's back, which quivers slightly, and every time it does it transmits its tremors to me. "My nice little tiger cub," I say, stroking it. I plan to give it mouth-to-mouth resuscitation.

(I don't want my sickness—the animal holed up in my guts—to die. We go hunting for it in this strange jeep, which is the analysis. The driver's seat is in the back because the analyst sits behind me, turning always to the left, to flush out and kill—guillotine—this beast. But just when the analysis is working and the beast is decapitated, I'm ready to give it mouth-to-mouth resuscitation in order to bring it back to life.)

Paul VI has arrived, this pope goes everywhere. This is an old dream, one of the first. My analysis lasted for three popes. This one has arrived by train, stopping at the station of a village near mine, and we're all there to greet him. He sticks his head out the window and smiles. My father and mother, who are both devout, rush up to him. He motions with his hand and calls my father, whispers something in his ear, gives him something. The train leaves and disappears, while all the people are still bowing down to the ground, as if worshipping my father, who is smiling. He then says, in a voice unlike his own, "The pope has said we can play," and I know that it's he and I who have to play. We play by shooting at each other. I'm the one who has to sit on the chair first. My father himself blesses the rifle that has been given to him by the pope, an American Garand, with eight rounds, semi-automatic. He aims. He fires. The bullet goes through my heart. I see my heart hanging there in the dawn. I complain to my father: "Look how you've pierced my heart." My father replies that I'd agreed to play. I raise a closed fist and compare it with my heart: they're the same size, but if he'd shot me in the fist, it would have hurt less. Now I'm supposed to shoot at him too, but I don't have a rifle that has been blessed. I take another look at my heart: the bullet went through it from right to left.

(This is a dream to which we often came back, and which we never stopped analyzing. Analysis of this dream of the heart was the heart of the analysis. Total understanding of even a single dream is possible only at the conclusion of the analysis, but the analysis is never concluded: life ends, and the analysis goes on. This dream means many things. Even in the most affectionate of family games, with the child sitting on his father's lap, the child expresses the desire for liberation, and the

129

*father responds by training him in repression. The pope—*il
papa—*has given my* papà *something that serves that very
purpose: to play, i.e., to love, by repressing, i.e., by killing.
The finest and most precise instrument for killing invented by
man is the Garand rifle. I used it as a soldier in Apulia, by the
sea. We lay on planks, each at his firing station, with the target
350 meters away. The Garand fires a single round, but as soon
as it has fired, it expels the shell and loads another cartridge in
the barrel. To fire again, you must pull the trigger again. This
mechanism serves to prevent the soldier from emptying his
whole clip when he sees the enemy: he is forced to fire one shot
at a time, but he doesn't have to reload his weapon, which
reloads itself. It is a powerful weapon: when I fired, the recoil
sent me sliding backwards on the planks, and a noncommis-
sioned officer, standing behind me, put one foot on my ass and
pushed me forward again. The Garand was introduced to us by
an instructor who held it up in his arms and began the lesson
by saying, "This is the finest and most precise weapon in the
world." Il* papa *gives this weapon to my* papà. *This weapon is
Catholicism. In the repression-liberation—i.e., training—
game between father and son, Catholicism is the most precise
instrument of repression in the world. What the father or
mother says to the child to repress him, as part of his upbringing, is felt in the dream as a blow to the most central part of the
child—the heart. The war between children and parents is a
war between those who need liberation in order to live and
those who need to see their own repression accepted and per-
petuated, in order not to die. On the repression side, the Garand or Catholicism is used; on the liberation side, one is struck
in the heart or closed fist. Heart and fist are alike: I raise heart
and fist and compare them. I can fire too, but my disadvantage
lies in the fact that I don't have a rifle that has been blessed:*

they fire with rituals, myths, saints, Christ, morality—in short, with the sacred—and we can fire with doubt. Therefore it turns out in the dream that they fire from the right: although hit in the back, when I hold up my heart to look at it, I see that the bullet has gone through it from right to left. As though he were on the right, and I on the left. Oddly enough, every time that in a dream the jeep of analysis came to a crossroads, it always turned left, with the result that it seemed to be going in circles. To go truly to the left, it would have to turn right once in a while.)

Moravia comes to see me, walking with his limping step. He smiles at me from a distance. He smells of perfume. I'm sitting on a dungheap, a pile of manure. Pasolini is also present, he gives me his hand and pulls me up. Then he disappears. Moravia and I walk together. We come to the Pantheon. "One could have oneself buried here," he says. I sniff. I've never liked the odor of the Pantheon, it smells of rot and dampness. "And where do you want to be buried?" asks Moravia, who is deaf. Because he's deaf, I don't reply in words, but bend down and pick up some straw (*paglia*) and put it in his hand, then I draw a wide circle with my arms, and finally move my legs as though I'm going up steps. By this I mean to say: "In Praglia, on the Euganean hills, in the courtyard of the Abbey, beside the staircase leading to the church." I sniff. There are pines and firs in front of that church, and the air is delightful. I wonder if Moravia has understood.

(This is a dream of death, but also about overcoming it, i.e., about immortality; it is also a comparison between Moravia, a bourgeois—perfumed—writer, and me, a writer from the proletariat, sitting on a dunghill. Pasolini pulls me up: it was he

who wrote the preface to my first novel and to my first poems. But Pasolini dies too soon, I remain alone with Moravia, and together we seek a reassuring hereafter. Moravia finds it in the Pantheon: his is a civic and layman's solution, but I conceive a solution not far from the religious one, while doubting that Moravia can understand it: he's always been completely deaf to these questions.)

We are at sea, on a two-masted fishing vessel. One mast is very tall and the other will be very tall, because it still appears to be growing. I ask my father, the owner of the boat, how much such masts cost. He tells me to figure it out for myself: seventy-five lire to the kilogram. I start calculating, estimating the mast at several tons. I get an enormous figure. I want to tell it to my father, but I see that he's crying, because the tall mast isn't there anymore, someone has cut it down. "It always happens," says my father, "and you never know who's done it." I'm worried because the smaller mast is creaking. "And what if they break it?" asks my younger son. "Bah," I say, "it always happens, and you never know who's done it." I want to cry but I can't, because I'm alone with my younger son and the ship is creaking.

(This, I suppose, is a dream about the transition from one generation to another: there's my father's generation, there's myself, there's my younger son. Life is a sailing ship, with a big mast and a small one; such masts cost huge sums, and nevertheless they are cut and discarded, by whom no one knows, let's say by history.)

I am the garbage collector for my apartment, stinking work that cannot be done by women, all of whom are perfumed. I keep collecting this garbage, which consists of cabbage stalks, sealing it in plastic bags, and throwing it through the proper opening into the garbage truck. As soon as I go back in the apartment, I find another pail of garbage ready, and this surprises me, since there's never anyone at home. Then I see other men collecting garbage, we're all there on the landing. Bah, obviously cabbages grow by themselves, and all the apartments are full of them.

(This is not an especially private dream, since it doesn't refer to something that happens in the dreamer's home, but in all homes. Refuse, waste, and garbage are produced in all of them. It may be possible to see in the dream some such concept as this: the consumer society means the consumption of people, but of the man more than the woman.)

We're in a tram. The conductor takes all the tickets, then asks for ours, my wife's and mine. In fact, we're the only ones left, everyone else has got off. The fare is twenty-five pieces per couple. My wife wants to pay with a single token, a plastic one at that, but instead of giving it directly to the conductor, she hands me her token so that I can pass it on to him. It's up to me to complete the fare. I add twenty-four small pieces of flesh, bits of salame, sausage, and fresh pork. Now that I've paid, I have nothing left, I'm desperate. The conductor puts the token in a drawer, which he opens by pulling it toward him and then closes by pushing it all the way back. He puts all the little pieces of flesh in a complicated mechanism consisting of a meat grinder, a discharge tube, a leveling blade, and a collection bag. The flesh is all ground up and comes out twisted and bloody, the leveling bar—a knife with the blade downwards—flattens it, from the discharge tube it drops into a black plastic bag that serves to collect it. "Damn it, it's not all there," I say, hoping the conductor will give me back a little. "It's there, it's there," he replies. He counts the pieces: "Twenty-three, twenty-four, twenty-five. Now you can ride. If you were alone, you'd ride for nothing."

(A nightmare—we have to open an air vent. I try to do it by myself. The flesh that I have to pay for the trip with my wife is repressed, unexperienced, sacrificed sexuality. "Flesh" is a common word for sexuality in all Catholic countries, from Western Europe to South America. The conductor is the superego, with his executioner's apparatus: meat grinder, blade, garbage bag. He transforms the fresh flesh I give him into dead and putrid meat, and this operation is the Catholic "mortification of the flesh." I don't understand the reason for such a precise number: twenty-five. I racked my brains over it for half a day, before going to the analytic session. Once there, I struggled with it until the end of the hour, without understanding why it should be exactly twenty-five. Just a minute before the end, I heard his armchair squeak, as it always did when he leaned toward me. "How old are you?" he asked. I told him. "And how many years have you been married?" I told him. "What's the difference between the first number and the second?" "Twenty-five." "All right"—and he stood up. The session was over. Blinded by this revelation, my feet staggering, I followed him to the door of the room, then along the hallway, and all the way to the front door. I didn't hear his goodbye. On my way home, I kept repeating: So that's what it was. Twenty-five years of my flesh being crushed and sliced and minced. Something inside me had counted those years one by one, and stored that number in my memory, keeping it ready to protest on the first occasion. This occasion was the analysis. I had remembered that number without knowing it. One paid twenty-five pieces of bleeding flesh for two people to make a

trip; if I'd been alone, I could have traveled for nothing. But traveling alone was the symbol of masturbation. Masturbation is tolerated, but sex for two is paid in blood.)

(Initially I had the habit of writing down my dreams so as not to forget them. I'd wake up at all hours, at three o'clock, at five, and by the light of a small flashlight write down my dream in a notebook. I'd go back to sleep. At dawn I'd wake up for good, read what I'd written, and wonder in astonishment: Who dreamt this? Sometimes the dream was so clear and detailed that it seemed impossible that I'd forget it. I wouldn't write it down. At dawn, I wouldn't remember a single word, person, or event from the dream: it had dissolved. I therefore decided never to trust myself, and always to write everything down. But even this was no guarantee, since his side of my ego was smarter than my side. I'd dream something and dream that I wrote it down: that I got up, turned on the flashlight, which flickered but finally shone, and felt warm in my hands. The wealth of details served precisely to convince me that this had occurred: the light had been lit, I had written, and could therefore go on sleeping. At dawn I roused myself in despair, like a customs guard who has failed to keep watch at the frontier: God knows who may have passed by that customs house and what he may have smuggled with him. I would show up for my analytic session as though on trial and expecting a guilty verdict. One day he said: "Writing down one's dreams is a symptom of obsession." I stopped writing them. The customs house became useless, as between two friendly countries, and to smuggle something across was no longer profitable.)

I make up my mind, pick up the phone, and call him. "Hello," I begin, "I'm the Marquis . . ."

(So am I a sadist? The Marquis de Sade was "divine," and I must say I take pleasure in the sobriquet.)

135

A woman sticks a banana in her vagina, meanwhile smiling with pleasure and showing her teeth. Then she removes the banana, peels it, and eats it with satisfaction.

(Perfect symbolism for the vagina dentata, which it's dangerous to enter. It is he who is the vagina, into which I'm afraid to enter: on the previous day I had begun the session by daring to ask him, "How are you?" while fearing that he would accept this familiarity and start talking about himself. He says, now, that I was not so much afraid of penetrating the vagina dentata as of penetrating the omnipotent figure of himself to see how it was made. "Anyway why would I be afraid of the vagina?" I ask. "Ever since I was little, I liked the idea of being born from there." "Yes," he says, "but here it's not so much a matter of coming out as of going in. And besides," he adds slowly, "the vagina dentata desecrates the memory of the vagina you loved," and I have the vague notion that one's reaction to the immorality of a female body is a reaction to the desecration of the mother's body.) (There is a connection between this dream and the previous one: penetration is always sadistic because it is an invasion of another's space, it means being inside someone else and outside oneself.)

I fly over a city in an airplane, the city is circular in shape, and at the center of the circle is a friar. This friar is worshipped, everyone touches his body, which stands tall on a pedestal, so that the heads of the people who come are on a level with his feet. His heart is below his navel, in the center of his body, and the point of the heart sticks out like a breast.

(This is a geometric dream, explaining why my city emerged around a saint and why my Sickness develops around the heart: Il Santo is the heart of Padua just as the heart is the

center of the body, and just as the mother is the heart of the heart. Strolling with my present sickness within the historical sickness of the city, I move like a current in the ocean: liquid in liquid.) (Man is a temporary neurosis in the chronic neurosis of History.)

I need to sleep, but there are three animals under the bed. I try to drive them out by using a rod resembling a radio antenna, with segments that telescope into each other. Three creatures come out, which to me look tame, but are actually wild beasts. One jumps on the bed, and wondering if it's a tiger, I defend myself with the rod; I have an anxiety attack.

(In recent days the Italian press has been discussing a new papal encyclical against the three forbidden sexual acts: pre-marital relations, homosexuality, and masturbation. One of these must concern me, because it's with me in my bed: the telescoping rod may indicate that it's the last one.)

I find myself in the vicinity of Il Santo, I go in on the right, and want to sit down in some pew in the shadows, but there's only a prie-dieu, well lighted, in the center. I settle myself there. In it there's a friar. "Are you on strike?" he asks me. I'm about to answer yes, but the confessor doesn't give me time, and begins to curse the strike. I'm astonished: a confessor who curses!

At that moment I find myself at some distance from the confessional—which is a cage, the kind used for tigers—sitting in a pew on the left, and the confessor is confessing a desperately contrite woman, who it seems to me ought to be forgiven in advance. In a loud voice he asks who condemns her. There are some small children present, and they all raise their hands as a sign of condemnation. I'm more astonished than ever. The confessor too raises his hand, and intones a mocking chant of triumph. I get up, walk all around the church, and go out on the left, but I don't know which way to go. A peasant, with a sickle in his hand, points out a road to me by waving the sickle, but in so doing he wounds his wrist. He curses too.

(A dream of abandonment: the loss of all guides. A church that takes a position against strikes is a church that "curses." It must be in some Bergman film that there's the scene of a witch burned at the stake while a chorus of children sings: it's a film about the Middle Ages, and seeing the scene again in a dream shows that I feel the church is still medieval. I go out on the left, but there's no place for me to go. Behind me, a church that curses; in front of me, a worker injured by his sickle, and who also curses: Catholicism and Communism as two blasphemies.)

I'm living in an apartment on the top floor, in a large building by the sea. From the sea my mother, who has only been dead for a short time, calls me. When they buried her, I had thought: How will she be able to call me from underground? That's why she calls me from the sea. Very pale, she rises from the water and comes toward me, I'm frightened, she has a cross in her hand, a huge white blinding cross. I have to close my eyes, even though I'm cutting wheat with a sickle, I go on cutting and wound my wrist, a lot of blood comes out. She comes close to me and takes the sickle from my hand, so that I'll stop cutting myself. She flies away like a UFO. I know that by using the sickle I can injure myself, but I must cut the wheat. I'm resigned to dying.

(I saw this mother as my earthly mother, he saw her more as the Mother Church, who wants to take the sickle from my

hand, it being a political symbol that makes me work in a way that seems like suicide. In reality, there's no conflict between the two interpretations: the Mother Church intervenes through the earthly mother. The dream's conclusion is that political involvement should be carried through to the end, suicide is no reason to stop.)

I come upon an archaeological site, perhaps in a scene from a Fellini film. Here there are ruins balanced on planks, and I climb up on one of these planks. In front of me is a hollow, a depression, and in it there must be a statue of red clay, a sphinx. As I approach, a loud-speaker somewhere screams at top volume: ". . . many years before Christ . . ." I cover my ears, have an anxiety attack, and wake up.

(It's a warning dream: something that has been buried is about to be excavated, something that goes back a long time. Its discovery is preceded by an anxiety attack, like every discovery, not only in analysis but also in history: even scientific and geographical discoveries are heralded by economic crises and accompanied by crises of adjustment.)

I'm unable to climb the stairs, I must have a heart murmur. I should go to a cardiologist. I go, I know him but don't recognize him, and he gives me an appointment at the Norcing Clinic, where he waits for me with scalpel in hand. The scalpel is a kitchen knife, or rather a screwdriver to unscrew me; it has a gleaming tip. We who are waiting are two or three pigs.

(The association that comes to me is that of Norcing with norcino, hog butcher; the analyst is perceived as someone who penetrates the heart with his tools, but those who need to go to him have a sense of guilt and feel like pigs.) (A curious and important detail: he made a mistake and said "pig" in the

139

singular, and I felt that at that moment he had slipped from my dream to the dream of some other patient unknown to me; he spoke of a heart that swelled with joy and contracted with sorrow, and I, who hadn't dreamt that detail, felt that in reality it fitted me very well; it was as though, standing at the same crossroads, I had taken one road and the unknown patient another, and both of us had used the analyst as an intermediary to communicate our mutual discoveries to each other; by responding to our associations with his associations, the analyst actually came to play this very role, connecting our unconsciouses with his unconscious and thus with all the unconsciouses connected with his. Each of us is a road, but he is a crossroads: by converging on him, we actually converge with many other roads.) (By mistake—luckily that day he was getting everything mixed up—he had used the word "sacred" along with "heart," and this certainly didn't apply to my case, since I had dreamt of a pig's heart; so someone else had dreamt of the "sacred heart," but if he had been able to slip from my dream to the dream of this unknown patient, it means that there were contacts between my dream and his, and that the two roads met at the same crossroads: having arrived at that crossroads, I looked along the other road, and saw at the end of it the Sacred Heart of Jesus, on the scarlet tunic. And for a moment I had an inkling that whoever first invented the Sacred Heart of Jesus had experienced a heart murmur, and had felt the need to go to a cardiologist. In short, it had been I, when I had arrived at the same crossroads centuries ago, and had taken the other road.) (The analytic relationship is a situation in which everything, including error, produces truth.)

It's Christmas, and Jesus is about to be born. Now he's been born, he's here. I wait to see how he'll sleep. It's important to take a close look at how the son of God goes to sleep on his first night on earth. And here's how he sleeps: he twitches, cries, wakes up, goes back to sleep, trembles. No doubt about it, it's a neurotic sleep. I don't know why, but I'm pleased by this discovery. I go away nodding my head approvingly: I'd like to give him a double dose of Flurazepam.

(This could be a dream about neurosis as sanctification, and vice-versa.)

The girl holds a tennis racquet in her hand, lifts it high, but it's not a racquet, it's a pair of oval pruning shears. I have a pole that keeps growing, and it's green. She challenges me to make it reach as far as the racquet. I succeed. With a snip of the shears she cuts my pole. Luckily it keeps growing and is still green. She squeezes the handle of the shears and cuts again.

I wonder how long this pole will keep on growing. There's a place called Palo Alto but I don't think it's ever been cut, I must tell her about it, it's called Palo Alto because it's never been cut, if it had been cut it would be called Palo Bajo: where does she want to go, to High Pole or Low Pole? If she wants to go to Low Pole, she'll have to go alone; if she wants to go to High Pole, then she shouldn't be cutting mine.

(This, I suppose, is a protest against the castrating aspects of feminism.)

We talk about this and that, while moving around the room. Then he takes of his jacket and remains in a bathing suit. He lies down on the bed. He has a very hairy chest, as I've always suspected, and this hair forms an empty nest. He keeps insisting on something or other, something mistaken, for example that there are only four volumes in the Encyclopedia. Instead there are more, many more, I tell him, making a gesture with my hand meaning "more," and at the same time I settle down in that nest, filling it.

(*This is a dream about the duration of the analysis: he had said at a certain point that four years might be enough, and I had replied that many more were needed. The dream says that from then on I began to perceive him as a nest, from which I had to be born. From that moment on my need to see what he is, how he is, to undress him, made itself felt: the analysis would be over once I had understood who he was.*)

Whenever I'm about to leave his house, I always have a sudden fear that the battery of my car has gone dead. As I turn on the ignition, I'm sad and trembling. Fortunately I can attach myself with a wire to a battery just behind the door in his house, a kind of supplementary battery that is not so much a battery as a battery charger: I attach the wires (which start from my navel) and my car starts up immediately, and the motor turns over beautifully because it's well lubricated. Now that I know this, I'm euphoric when I turn the ignition.

(*Naively or ironically, the dream perceives an auto-analysis as an analysis carried out in an auto. This analysis cannot start unless it receives a charge from him. It would seem that my relationship with him is now reduced to this: to receive a charge in order to depart with my auto, that is, for auto-analysis.*)

I'm fed up with traveling by car, from now on I'll take the train. Everybody travels by train, each with his or her little suitcase. Each has a berth. I get undressed and get under the covers. I'm wearing only a jersey that reaches my groin, and no undershorts. There are boys and girls in the compartment. We're all reading. The girl next to me is wearing a transparent nightie, elegant and black, its border embroidered in white with a Greek-style pattern that looks like this: ⊔⌐⊔⌐⊔⌐⊔. I'm wearing this short woolen jersey with no underpants, my penis shows but it doesn't bother me, to me it seems elegant. The conductor comes and asks for tickets. I have a discount ticket and must therefore show my I.D., besides we all have I.D.'s, I look at those of the others and read the inscription: PO-AR-RE-TOU. They are made of light plastic and must be welfare passes. Mine is inscribed $\Psi\alpha$, and it seems to me that when he sees it, the conductor makes the gesture of raising his cap.

(The initials $\Psi\alpha$ were the private abbreviation used by Freud in his letters to signify "psychoanalysis." The other cards may be perceived as poorer, less valid; it may also be that the abbreviations, taken individually, have a meaning, for example: Politics, Art, Religion, Tourism.)

It's not clear whether it's a celebration for *L'Unità* or *Il Manifesto*, since all the newspapers now hold organized celebrations. There are tables for eating, with sections that serve healthy food and sections that serve polluted food. Indeed, for some reason or other, almost everyone is eating in the polluted sections. I go to a healthy table, carrying with me a stick that I could also use as a clothes rack, since there aren't any there. The cooks in the healthy section are women, and they're preparing a minestrone. They take my stick and put it in this minestrone, then taste it and nod to show that it's good. They invite everyone to eat. I too taste it with a spoon, but they pull me away and start hitting everybody, they don't want anyone to eat. They take dry grass and throw it in the minestrone, which now becomes a kind of mash of hay for animals, and so I go away hungry, beaten up, and without my clothes rack.

(I felt it as a dream about sexuality: sexuality is natural, joyous, forbidden, necessary, healthy, dirty, for everyone, impossible, and punished.)

It's Christmas and in every household the head of the family writes a poem. Christmas is a kind of literary contest. My wife is sulking because I haven't yet written my poem. But the fact is that I can't get it to rhyme. Finally I write: "It's Christmas yet—and we're in debt." She's offended, and says that the poems of other families are much better. She cries, and I'm filled with anxiety.

(Christmas is a holiday of the bourgeoisie, not of the Church: a spending spree in which everyone is forced to compete, because in every household the wife and children are the fifth column of the consumer society.)

There's a nasty schoolteacher who asks, "How much is one and one and one?" A little boy answers, "Three." The teacher cuffs him and says, *"Nein, nein,* four," and holds up four fingers. The boy takes note of it and writes four, and besides this teacher can't be wrong because he's a saint.

(This is an anxiety dream, a recurring nightmare. It reflects the situation of someone who knows he's right, but must deem it proper to be wrong. The day before I had this dream I'd read that the SS, at Auschwitz, kept a numerical count—not a list of names—of persons who died, and if a pregnant woman died they counted her as two. So one plus one plus one can make four, and besides it's impossible for the SS to be wrong, since "God was with them." The anxiety produced by the dream

probably emerged from the commingling of Catholicism and Nazi-Fascism, that is to say, of my mother with the jailers, of my people with its enemies, of those who loved me the most with those who did the greatest harm.)

Essentially the pope is an engraver, and works in copper. He has a press with a pink symbol representing a rose. Under the rose is inscribed in handwritten characters, "*Recisa rinascit*," followed by the signature, a trumpet blast, "ta-tara-tata." This pope engraves copper plates, prints four hundred copies on his press, and then scatters them to the four winds.

(The new pope, Wojtyla, has issued his first encyclical. He worked on it by himself, like an artist. When he finished it, he sent it to the four corners of the globe. The motto of this pope actually contains many t's: "Totus tuus, amo te.")

I'm returning from a town in Germany, driving full-speed in my car. In every village I steal something, possibly copper carafes. I make people lie down on the ground and calmly put a pistol to their heads. I'm inflexible. The people lying on the ground cough from the dust, they're thirsty. When I leave, a shepherd, who has just milked his herd, gives the Germans milk to drink, and I'm a little puzzled.

(A friend once said to me, "When I hear German spoken, I speed up." During their retreat, the Germans stole everything in our house, yard, and stable; my father sat on the ground, weeping with rage, while a German kept guard over him by aiming a pistol at his ear. I looked attentively at this pistol that sufficed to keep my papà immobilized, and that had a little cylinder on the left side near the butt: I tried to understand how it was made so that as soon as I grew up, I could make myself one like it and go to Germany to avenge

my father. Now instead the new pope, the shepherd, was go-
ing to Germany on a journey of reconciliation, and this I
couldn't swallow.)

I write many letters, in the hope that someone will
deliver them to my wife. I'm about to die, I have heart
disease, I must write these letters and keep looking in
the inkwell, afraid I'll find it empty. And besides, as
long as I write I won't die, and therefore I write as long
as possible.

(The day before I had read Aldo Moro's letters, which had
just been published. The identification with Moro is encour-
aged by many things: moro *is a dialect word for "boy," since*
all boys around here have dark hair; Moro was shot in the
heart, as was I—I mean as happened to me in the dream of the
Garand rifle; he was killed by the Red Brigades, and no one
knows quite what they are.) (He remarks that by introducing
ever more powerful figures—Moro, the pope, many popes—
I'm "raising my sights," like the Red Brigades.)

The bell rings, it's the mailman, I go downstairs. The
mailman, for fear of letter bombs, brings the mail in a
galvanized metal box. Every so often a letter goes poof,
splits open, and sprays the mailman with white flour.
Indeed, he's white all over. Now he's going to give me
my package, let's hope it doesn't go poof. But it's not a
package, it's a small rectangular box, like those for choc-
olates. It gives off a smell of incense.

(One out of ten of us in this city has been threatened, by
letter or telephone, from right or left: teachers, manufacturers,
trade union members, politicians, priests, students. Yesterday
I received another threatening letter from the right-wing group
Ordine Nuovo: all it contained was a drawing of a coffin, the
color of chocolate. I noted that a Latin cross was drawn on the

coffin, and a Greek cross under the signature "Ordine Nuovo,"
next to the fasces with the ax at the top.)

I have a nice apartment, no question about it, on the
top floor, sunny and well-lighted. Friends stop by for a
drink, I keep bottles just for them. But someone wishing
me ill has left a very large cross, which takes up the
whole hallway, so that in whatever direction I move I
must always step over this cross. At a certain point I
pick it up and put it in a corner, then scrape it with a
rasp, and I see that the cross shrinks in size, until in the
end it becomes a kind of dagger with a hilt. Then I
realize that whoever brought it here won't show up
again, because I'll be able to defend myself with the very
weapon he has given me.

(When my father left for the war, along with everyone else
who had been called up from around our village, a celebration
was held, during which the priest blessed the soldiers. A month
later the priest received a letter enclosing a photograph, which
showed a group of Slavs who had been shot in Istria. The
soldier who had sent the photo had written underneath it
"Thou shalt not kill," and the priest hid the letter, but his
hands were trembling as he folded it.) (This memory re-
emerged from the void immediately after the dream. It had been
so completely erased that I still don't know whether it was a
memory or a fantasy.)

I'm all wet with urine, somebody has pissed on me.
It's useless to try and find him, he's nowhere to be seen.
All I can do is dry myself.

(Yesterday, lying on the couch, I felt the place still warm.
Whoever had had the hour before mine had just left. I had the
feeling that he'd sweated, perhaps had an anxiety attack. At
first I wondered whether or not to mention it to the analyst,

whether to discuss it or not. Then I decided not to talk about it, without understanding why. At that moment I remembered that when my father was at the front, we brothers slept in one bed and our sisters in another. Sometimes, out of fear, anxiety, or illness, one of my brothers would wet the bed, and on waking up would implore me, "Don't tell anyone," because a little girl who wets the bed gets comforted, while a little boy gets punished. When our father came back, we told him boastfully that the little girls sometimes had wet the bed while thinking of him, but we never told him that his sons had done the same.)

I'm in the hospital, and when the doctors come to examine me, they don't use a thermometer but an odor-ometer: every pain produces a smell. They put it on my navel and then check the readings.

(This dream came right after the previous one. As a child, during the war, when I woke up at dawn and smelled urine in the room, I realized immediately that one of my brothers or sisters had been more sick than usual during the night. The years when we were without our father were years of urine-anxiety. Something here is connected with renal colic and the blood in my urethra.)

I'm watching a John Wayne film on TV while holding a cat in my arms, the cat is asleep and feels heavy. I have this weight on my heart. John Wayne shoots his pistol and smiles with a crooked mouth that opens more on the right than the left.

I have this weight on the heart, but they remove it with a surgical operation, they roll me swiftly into the operating room and cut away this weight—a plastic bag—with a razor blade, I emerge very slowly, feeling light and with the strange sensation that anxiety and speed, calm and immobility, are pairs of similar things.

(One of my problems is speed: traveling swiftly gives me anxiety, speed heightens my moral problems. That's how it was for my peasant mother: to go anywhere by car created psychological problems for her, the same ones that an airplane creates for me. It almost seems that where there is no physical fatigue, there must be moral fatigue, and where there is neither one nor the other, there is the malady that the Greeks called fatigue. Only traveling in a natural environment—dirt roads, people on foot, no traffic signals, much fatigue but no danger— only such a journey was happy and natural, all others were unnatural, rapid, and disturbed. That's all I can say.) (The cat lies on my heart; the heart is a vulnerable organ, an external organ, a defensive organ; our real heart, which lies within us and is defended at all costs, is the nervous system.)

His chest is very hairy, and the hair forms a nest. I fly away from this nest, then come back to his chest, which is very hairy, and the hair forms a nest. I fly away from this nest. Then come back.

(This is a dream about the beginning of healing: my attempts, albeit failures, to take flight are insistently repeated. The repetitive way in which I happen to tell this dream is explained by the fact that on the previous evening I had been listening to a broken record, which never got to the end because the needle kept getting stuck in the groove. The end of the analysis is like that: the analysis seems to be over, there's nothing more to say, one talks about prices in the stores, automobile repairs, newspaper articles, and still one never finishes, a malevolent mechanism keeps it from reaching its true end.)

This is not the first dream about healing; actually the first minute of analysis is already a step toward healing, because it provides the following sensation: the Sickness, which before was all on one side, is now divided in two; the closer the union of the two, the more perfectly divided is the sickness. In the phase of the analysis in which this dream occurred, however, many other dreams that can be said to be about healing occurred as well. In reality, man is a sickness, and for him there is no cure from the sickness called man. A man goes into analysis not to be healed, but to find out why he is going into analysis. These dreams of healing showed the analyst sleeping, with his hairy chest, the hair woven into a nest, and the nest empty: I had flown away. Or else they showed my car arriving at his house, parked there with the motor idling, and when I got back in departing swiftly and smoothly: while once I had to connect my battery with his battery charger inside the house, now the motor was constantly on, I never even needed my own battery. As I've already said, it's my impression that with this dream (which indicates perfectly how the analysis ends: the analysis ends by not ending) his side of my ego was making fun of my side, in this joking fashion: it spoke of auto-analysis as an analysis carried out with or in an auto. It wasn't the first time it had done this, but now it did it more often. Essentially, the end of the analysis was marked by an exchange of joking remarks between his side of my ego and my side, which had become friends after his side had lost much of its power and my side had gained it, and they thus found themselves more or less on an equal level.

PART FOUR

1. The signature

The first rule of analysis (to say everything that comes to mind) is inapplicable, because it requires too many unfeasible communications. There's no limit to what comes to mind, while what one technically succeeds in saying is always very little. But the fact that there's a limit to speaking should not be a limit to what can be said. Analysis is to man as a civil war is to the State. It may happen—indeed, it always happens—that in a civil war fighting does not take place in all the public squares, but the State cannot presume to ask that some squares be exempted: if it did, all the rebels would take refuge in those squares, and at a certain point it would discover that those very squares it wanted to preserve intact were infested by the enemy, and would have to destroy them.

The same thing happens if one goes into analysis saying, "I'll talk about everything except my wife, or my children, or my work, or my mother." He'll end up having to talk only about what he didn't want to mention.

The inability to say everything is not a sickness, it is *the* sickness, from which other sicknesses derive: the stomach, heart, or intestines may seem to be sick, but in reality what is sick is the tongue. Language is the connection between child and mother, and by extension between man and everything. Therefore, in reality, it is this connection that is sick. Since language is a connec-

153

tion, this sickness is epidemic: we live immersed in sickness, and transmit it by transmitting language. Language is the virus of the sickness called man. The more man becomes man and differentiates himself from animals, the sicker he gets. All this is what we call progress. The animal is not neurotic and knows no progress. There is a pride in neurosis, which coincides with the pride in being human. There is a contempt for the non-neurotic that coincides with the contempt for the subhuman. This pride in being oneself, and the refusal to be other than oneself, are the chief stumbling blocks to recovery, that is to say, to analysis.

To become other than oneself is an expression that should be taken literally. After seven years of analysis, I don't speak the words I spoke before; I don't live as before; I don't eat or write as before. The expression "I don't write as before" should be taken literally: my handwriting is totally different. There is a connection between morale, words, and handwriting. The moment this connection was broken, my handwriting was fragmented. I had always written with the letters hooked together, as though encased in the tunnel of the line, and my script was the exact graphic equivalent of the animal caged in the tunnel of my guts. When this tunnel was opened up and aired, my handwriting became disconnected, and the letters separated from each other as though I were writing in a monosyllabic language. My signature was unrecognizable, even to myself. If someone had shown me a check or promissory note with my new signature, I would never have been able to say whether it was true or forged.

I'd draw my salary at the Banca d'Italia, where before

receiving cash you have to sign a receipt. The atmosphere is already tense, we're massed in a single room, queued up at various tellers' windows in such a way that a pair of guards, with submachine guns (paratrooper model) slung across their shoulders, can control us all: if they wanted to, they could mow us all down from the first window to the last with a single volley. Women, unfamiliar with firearms, are always afraid they'll go off by themselves. Old men, having fought in wars, are rejuvenated at the sight of firearms; they feel secure and stand in line with their newspapers open in their hands. To love firearms is right-wing. Scratch an Italian and you find a fascist. Children are spellbound at the sight of these soldiers in their black berets and uniforms the color of steel, who are stationed at our backs, their legs spread, with one hand steady on the butt of their guns as though ready to open fire. The teller asks everyone for identification, presents the receipt, waits for the signature, checks it, and then pays by sliding the money under the glass.

I was the only person who had to repeat my signature more than once and supply proof of identity: if I was myself, if I was known, and by whom. I reached the window, was given the form, signed it, and gave it back. The teller looked at the signature and was perplexed: it bore no resemblance to the specimen signature they had on file. So he had me sign again. I took the form and wrote another signature, which in its turn did not even vaguely resemble the one written a minute before. The teller shook his head and went to call his supervisor. My companions in the line became impatient. The teller returned with the supervisor: "Documents."

155

I pulled out all the documents I had, and passed them under the glass. All were signed, but none of the signatures corresponded to the one I'd just written. Again they gave me the receipt. I looked around, to right, to left, behind me. The guard was at my back, grasping his submachine gun with both hands. It's a short-barreled, rapid-fire weapon. By now I'm very nervous and would rather postpone the matter until tomorrow, but I doubt that it's possible. I sign again. The ballpoint trembles in my fingers, the signature is incorrect even from the standpoint of spelling: it's as though I didn't know my own name, and when asked "What's your name?" had answered "Ferdindo Larrio." The supervisor is dismayed and says, "Come to my office."

I'm worried, clearly I won't get a lira of my salary. We go inside to his office.

I had never been in that part of the bank. Beyond the main room, with its tellers' windows for the public, was a series of tiny little cells like a monastery, and on the front of each cell a nameplate with the name and title of the friar who worked inside it.

I immediately have the strange sensation that there's a connection between guarding money and guarding the Sacrament, but I don't have time to reflect on it, since we're already there, here's the supervisor's office, a little cell with a tiny window and a small open door through which you get a glimpse of a toilet bowl. So it's a W.C. The supervisor closes the door, and the toilet bowl vanishes.

I almost have the feeling that the supervisor's career (from teller to overseer of tellers) is symbolized by the acquisition of that physical convenience, a private toilet.

The guiding objects of a career, from the Stone Age to our day, are always the same: one's own body and its appendage, the body of one's woman. And it occurred to me that when they'd called this man, he wasn't in his office, he was there in the toilet: he'd hurried out and forgotten to close the door. Leaving his office on his way to me, he may still have been buttoning his pants. Because these good bourgeois types don't wear pants with zippers, but with buttons: it's more traditional, and those who achieve a little power immediately latch onto tradition, since the acquisition of new power makes up for past impotence. Good, now we know with whom we're dealing.

He realizes that I've understood, and tries to blot out my discovery by closing the door of the W.C. But now it's too late, nothing can belie what I know, and all he does by making that gesture is to underscore it. He's uneasy, and doesn't know how to begin. He asks me to write my signature, telling me to be calm, it's a pure formality. I'm extremely calm, if he wants a signature I'll write it. There. It's a firm, upright signature, and looks like all the signatures on my documents. It's my signature, I am I.

He's perplexed, sitting there with the papers in his hand, a poor old man with a bald skull and hardening of the arteries, who has consumed his whole life in order to have a toilet in which to defecate and urinate in peace, maybe he has trouble micturating, the enlarged prostate presses on the urethra and cuts it off, he urinates drop by drop, the effort makes the bladder thicken and become cancerous, all old men have cancer of the bladder, it's not dangerous or painful. Paul VI had it too. Anyway if he wants another signature, I'll write it. There. And still another. Now he has to give me my salary. It's the end of the month and I have a right to it.

I stand up, he's surprised and remains seated. He looks up at me, I look down at him. I'm sure that if I lean forward a little, I'll be able to see whether he ever finished buttoning his fly. I lean forward a little, he looks worried. He takes a piece of paper, writes something on it, and hands it to me. I look at it, it says: "Pay the amount of his salary to Mr. . . ." and there's my name. I read it again. In my surname there's an *m*, which he hasn't written clearly, it looks like an *n*. I take the ballpoint and add a stroke, now it's all right. He's astonished, I think he'd like to apologize. But never mind, I'm in a hurry and leave. Besides, when we're nervous, or there's someone with a submachine gun behind us, or our fly is open in public, our handwriting may feel the effects. When then we come out of analysis, our handwriting changes forever, but this he doesn't know, no one knows it. I go back down, hand the note to the teller, who reads it a couple of times, looks disappointed, slides the money to me under the glass, I leave, the guard follows me with his gaze, he's disappointed too, it seems to bother him that everything is normal.

2. Death of a partisan

From time to time during my analysis, a memory would come back to me that I didn't know how to place. It came back so often I could place it everywhere. I'll try to tell it.

When I was a child, I'd sometimes see soldiers departing for the war. A pair of carabinieri on motorcycles would come looking for them, bringing the call-up notice, and they had to leave immediately. Some left as volunteers, and therefore dressed differently from the others: they put on black shirts. All of them, before leaving, went to church to receive a blessing. I had little idea of what the war was about, or who was the enemy, but there was no doubt that God was on our side. A few years later an incident occurred in our village that was to have extraordinary importance for my moral education: a partisan, captured by the fascists, was about to be shot. He had been flushed out by dogs during a dragnet operation, had hidden in a ditch, but the barking dogs sniffed out his presence from afar and began closing in on him, and he had to jump out and climb a tree. Standing upright among the branches, he kept his hands raised. Once they'd caught him, they took him to the village square, and held him there for half a day, crouching next to a low wall, so that everyone could get a look at him. Nobody could identify him, he wasn't from our village. I was six or seven years old, and he was the first

159

partisan I'd ever seen. I expected him to be stronger. I thought partisans were athletes, because they were always on the run. Instead, this one was very weak. He sat slumped against the wall as though he didn't have the strength to get up. I kept thinking: Now he'll jump up and run away.

But he never ran away. A fascist, submachine gun in hand, stood guard over him, walking back and forth and smoking. Now and then he stopped beside him, leaned over and blew smoke in his face, or took the cigarette butt and burned his nose, the nose from which I was later to bleed. I thought: Now he'll get up and punch him in the face. Instead—strange—he just blinked his eyelids, as though his eyes hurt him, and stayed where he was. To hit the fascist, he would have had to move his arms. Instead, his arms remained limp and dangling, as though they weren't arms at all, but the empty sleeves of an amputee.

A jeep with a loudspeaker had made the rounds of all the local villages, announcing that at five in the afternoon a bandit, an enemy of the Italian people, would be executed in the square. The jeep was full of men in black shirts, which made me think they'd been blessed—they probably had been—and had some connection with my mother and father, they were our men, and the captured bandit was one of our enemies. At five o'clock they get ready for the execution. All of them are nervous because not enough people have come out to watch. They stand the prisoner up against the wall, but he slides back down to the ground. So they leave him there. Now the priest arrives. He goes up to the prisoner, speaks to him a little in a low voice, but the man doesn't respond. Then the priest straightens up, and with his crucifix makes the sign of the cross over him, and this leaves me confused: why does he first bless the blackshirts, who are our men, and now bless a partisan, who is their enemy? He does everything calmly, with precision. A fascist runs over and tries to push him away, another fascist detaches himself from the firing squad and also comes to lead the priest away, but the priest is in no hurry, and still holding the crucifix in his hand, he moves a couple of meters to the partisan's right, stops, raises his arm, and points the crucifix at the little squad of fascists who are preparing to fire. It almost looks as though they're going to fire at him. Now they'll fire. The partisan has watched the scene without emotion, as though not even seeing it. In my memory the episode ends here, before the actual shooting of the partisan. But I've learned that these lapses of memory often conceal a presence: the shooting took place, but changed nothing, because the partisan remained just as he was, crouching on the ground with his head down and his arms limp, so you couldn't even tell whether he'd been hit or not; it was like shooting at a pile of rags. That vision, of a man dying as though he were a pile of rags, without a complaint, without a twitch, without a jolt, was the most terrifying part of the whole scene, which is why I erased it from my memory so that not a trace remained. But there's another proof to remind me that the scene took place the way I witnessed it. One of the films about the Vietnam war shows a Vietcong being captured by a South Vietnamese patrol, brought to a village controlled by the Americans, thrown on the ground against a wall, and shot. When I saw this film,

I said to myself a moment before the shooting: I bet he won't move. They shoot, and he doesn't move. But I know he died, because I'd seen the scene before. They used the Garand to shoot him, the finest and most precise weapon in the world. Whoever directed that scene in the film had seen the killing of my partisan.

History is a crime. Man is the corpus delicti. Analysis is history on trial.

3. The last of the magician

Analysis had brought to the surface a great number of episodes from my childhood and adolescence of which I had perhaps never been aware. They emerged, glowed, and vanished. Like fireworks. The pretext that had drawn them forth could be very tenuous, at times invisible. When in the first months of analysis I began to speak of my mother, who had just died, I used to wave my left arm in the air, seemingly as a rhetorical gesture, like someone underscoring his remarks with body language, but in reality in an effort to grasp hold of her. I was floundering about in the void. Analysis is a journey among ghosts. At the end of the analysis, seven years later, one day when I was at a loss for something to say and went on waving my left arm in the void, I started talking about my mother again. I'm sure it was this movement of my arm that evoked her memory.

To the left and slightly behind me, however, it was not really the void. It was he. And this backward groping was also an attempt to grasp hold of him, to pull him into my problems and keep him there, to use him as a rope to climb out of them.

I was lying down, feeling heavy and empty-headed. I was anxious. I waited. When one begins a session by waiting, danger lies—as I learned with time—at the threshold of twenty minutes: if the first twenty minutes go by without a word, most likely you won't speak at all. After twenty minutes, he's earned the right to tend to his own affairs, he's writing notes, perhaps for a lecture that he'll give after supper. In that last five-minute interval between fifteen and twenty minutes, I cross my legs, put my hands under my neck, look at the ceiling, turn my head to the right (where there's a blank wall, but in one corner there's a spot of moisture that with a little imagination looks like an airplane in a nose dive; each time I looked at it, I'd wonder: What kind of plane is it? a Zero? a Spitfire?), turn it to the left (where there's the bookshelf, with its sets of complete works, but there was always a volume missing from the works of Freud, I'd look to see which one and think: Volume Three is missing. Ah, so you're rereading *The Interpretation of Dreams*? Good, you've been a little weak lately), take a deep breath, sigh, and search for an excuse to begin. He sits behind me in total silence, without rustling papers, without writing, without shifting in his chair, and for all I know he could have gone out for a snack. I'd wait, moving my left arm behind me in the air. I wasn't thinking of anything.

"You're looking for something with your hand," he said all of a sudden.

I wasn't expecting it. Among other things, it was against the rules for him to speak first, and he'd never done so before. (The end of the analysis was marked by a progressive breaking of the rules.) Anyway it was an excuse, and I had to seize it.

"Yes, I was looking for her," I replied.

"Her . . . or me?" he asked.

The question surprised me. Actually my answer was

ambiguous, because in speaking of my mother, I often referred to her simply as "her" (*lei*), and since I used the formal "you" (also *lei*) in addressing him, he had probably more than once sensed a certain ambiguity in my speech. Now I discovered it. The ambiguity was not only in my words. It was in everything, it was myself. Sometimes I would tell him about some very embarrassing gaffe that I'd made, especially in relation to him (describing, for example, a dream in which he had not cut a good figure: he had just given a lecture, and I dreamt that throughout it he'd kept his mouth open without making a sound, like a statue in Pompeii, meaning that he'd had nothing to say). To make amends, I expressed my contrition, insisting on my great esteem for him. On his side, silence. On mine, mortification. Then his chair creaked and I heard his voice saying softly, "Very funny."

Yes, I was laughing, while trying not to, and hoping he wouldn't notice. He had noticed. I might as well laugh out loud. I did.

"Hilarious."

When he interpreted some offensive dream, after the first words I realized in a flash what he was driving at, what the dream meant, and my reaction was to cross my legs, uncross them, cross them again. He'd interrupt his explanation for a moment to comment, "You'd like to leave."

Yes, I would have liked to leave, I didn't want to hear him tell me these things, but it couldn't be helped. Nailed to that couch, listening to him tell me out loud, from half a meter away, the most unpleasant truths, and paying him at the same time, I thought how nice it would be to have one's analysis by telephone: he talks to you while you make faces at him.

In the first sessions, I was ashamed of the noises of my body. My hour was in the early afternoon, right after the midday meal. On my way, I'd stop for a coffee, and then arrive at his place with my stomach full, my digestion in progress, and my tongue thick. It was hard to start talking. Long silence. In the silence, my stomach sometimes made itself heard. I was aware of it in time, but there was no way to hold it back: it started far down, and came out as a long drawn-out rumbling of the bowels. Embarrassed, I tried to smother the sound by matching it with another: I scraped one shoe against the other, breathed heavily, shifted my position on the couch to make the springs creak. Nothing—that vulgar rumble remained the only sound to be heard, surrounded by half an hour of silence. I thought: Now I bet he'll make some remark about that noise.

He said nothing, but if he'd known how ashamed I felt, he surely would have spoken. But his belly also made itself heard: sometimes in those same long, anguished silences, you could hear the noisy movement of chewed food in his stomach. I'd think: Now he'll drown out this sound with something else, let's see what he comes up with. I envied him because he could pick up a book, bang it on the table, rustle the pages, move a pencil, lean over to pick up a piece of paper, make his chair squeak. He had possibilities that were denied to me. I waited. Nothing, he did nothing: the noise in his belly persisted, isolated and total. Amazed, I said to myself: So it's all right. I stopped trying to cover up my noises, and then it would happen that my stomach rumbled, and his would reply, while we ourselves were silent. A large portion of those early-afternoon sessions went by like this, with these prehistoric messages between our intestines.

I began the analysis in September, and by November he already had a cold. I could hear his voice becoming nasal, and was afraid he'd get sick and have to interrupt the sessions. Inside of me I protested: So take care of yourself! Do you have an inhalator? Do you want to borrow mine? As soon as he opened his mouth, there at the door, I listened to the timbre of his voice to see if it sounded natural, calculated whether the illness had progressed or not, and concluded: Maybe he'll be all right, he's stronger than he looks. This feeling, like a somewhat more open smile than usual on his part, or a rumble in his belly that lasted longer than mine, was enough to make me euphoric for a week. No one will understand me.

I was very slow in getting on familiar terms with him. For years I gave the analysis a technical and professional tone, it was his job, I was paying him for it, and that was that. I knew absolutely nothing about his private life. Once I had an automobile accident (but not while I was on my way to him), and since the car was not fixed in time, I had to miss a session and informed him by telephone. The next time we saw each other, I talked about something quite different, told him my dreams, and he seemed surprised. He paused, but accepted the game, and entered into an explanation of the dreams that took up the whole hour. But at the end of the session he looked resentful, almost hurt, and it seemed to me that the smile with which he said goodbye was less open than usual, as though he were reproaching me: You don't consider me a friend, and yet I suffer for you.

Months later, I find a wrecked car in his courtyard. Christ, I thought, he's dead! I ring. Footsteps. The door opens. It's he. He greets me in the way that means: Come up and come in. I go in, feeling elated. I lie down and tell him I was afraid it was he who had had that accident.

"No," he says, "not I."

A pause.

I feel sad. He doesn't live alone: maybe someone who lives with him was killed. To hell with analyzing dreams, there's a dead person in the house, one can't ignore it.

"It's not your wife?" I ask. "Your son?"

A pause. So I've hit the target. I know nothing of his wife, but I know he's married. I know nothing of his son, but I know he has one. In certain sessions that had gone by in absolute silence, I'd occasionally heard what sounded like a child riding a bicycle or tricycle in a distant room, and I distinctly hear, I meant heard (but I hear it even now), the jingling of a bell. A child was racing around on his bicycle and ringing the bell attached to the handlebars. Sometimes he didn't brake in time and banged into the wall with the wheels, and I heard a woman's voice scolding him without anger. I cannot express what I felt, I'd crashed against one of those boundaries that define the structure of man, and beyond which man is no longer himself but something else. I'll try to say it. Hearing that child racing in his room with his little bicycle, I'd listen for the whole hour, letting myself be invaded by a sentiment that if translated into words would be: Our child. May those who are capable of it understand me.

I never saw the mother of our child, but I heard her voice a few times on the telephone. She knew about me, just imagine a wife not knowing about her husband's life. I'd say, "Today I'll be fifteen minutes late," and she'd reply, "I'll let him know." She was a good wife, affectionate and understanding, with a warm, enveloping voice. Maybe a little on the plump side, which I like.

Was she dead? And the child? Were they in that car? Silence.

I jump up and turn around. He's astonished. He takes the pipe out of his mouth and stares at me.

"Has something happened to your wife? your child?"

He looks at me thoughtfully. My reaction has caught him by surprise. He takes his time. "No, neither of them," he says slowly, reflects a moment, then adds, "It's not our car."

I try to understand, and I get this explanation: it's an accident involving strangers, they hadn't known where to leave their now unserviceable car and had asked if they could leave it in the courtyard.

"In any case," he concludes, "if it serves to make our conversations more friendly, and since nobody got hurt, this accident is welcome."

So he had expected me to express an interest in him and his family. But I'd wanted nothing else, it was just that I hadn't dared. I never dared enough with him. In seven years, I never called him by name. And yet there were hours of such total intimacy that at the end of the session, when I tried to go over what had been said, I was unable to extricate my words from his. I remembered exactly the sequence of thrusts and parries, but I was no longer able to tell whether I had uttered the thrust and he the parry, or vice-versa. An embrace is much less close than this fusion. It is not a fusion, it's a substitution of one for the other. I felt that I could call him *tu*, but I never did. I still have a faint suspicion that if I had, the analysis would have been over much sooner.

Now he even telephoned my house sometimes. If he didn't reach me, either because I was home alone or there wasn't anyone there, he'd leave a message on the answering machine. When I returned, I'd play the tape of the answering machine and listen to the voice of whoever had called. The first time I heard his voice—strange—I didn't recognize it at first. And yet his recorded voice was the same as his real one. When I came to the end of the message, I said to myself calmly: But it's he. I played the tape again, not to hear the message again, but his voice. It was his voice, exactly. Why had it never aroused any emotion in me? I played it once more. It was the voice I knew so well, unmistakable and always present. It had not aroused my emotions because I'd never stopped hearing it. It was a constant voice inside me. I lived without interruption in the company of that voice. A moment before hearing it on the tape, I was already hearing it. That's why it hadn't surprised me. I erased the whole tape except for that message, so that I could listen to it again from time to time. He pronounced his *o*'s very closed. I tried to imitate him, looking for words with a lot of *o*'s. Dividing the syllables, I intoned: "U/gó Fó/scó/ló."

During the first year he never telephoned, from the second year on only occasionally, in the last two once a month, in the last months once a week. I'd go home, play the tape, and say to myself: Let's hear what the magician has to say today. I'd got in the habit of calling him the magician, partly as exorcism, partly as a joke. I'd listen to the message (he was asking me to come twenty minutes later than usual, because earlier he couldn't make it—he never said why; he was asking me to cancel Wednesday and come on Saturday instead—he never furnished an explanation) and mark it on my calendar. The first years I always obeyed, rearranging my days so as to conform to his new requirements. In the end it was he himself who wanted to know if I had any commitments that would be upset by a possible change in schedule, and when I enumerated them, he said never mind, let's keep the original appointment. So this gave me the idea that his requirements were less serious than my commitments. He tended to suggest a change in schedule more frequently. I began to object. I preferred to miss a session rather than go at a time when I had an important engagement. One day something happened that I would never have thought possible: I'd accepted a change and was supposed to go on Saturday, but since I'd almost never gone on Saturday before, I forgot. Monday comes and he asks me why I hadn't at least telephoned him if I hadn't been able to make it on Saturday. What surprised me was not the fact that I'd forgotten, but that I'd missed an appointment without being in the least aware of it. Then I realized that it was the beginning of the end of the analysis.

In the first months, the loss of a session was a dramatic event. He would let me know in time, two or three weeks in advance. At first the news left me cold: with two or three weeks still to go, the thing didn't bother me. Gradually as the days went by, all my attention was focused on that loss. During the session before it, I talked of nothing else: I tried to foresee the effects of this absence in order to cancel them out. I never succeeded. The day on which we were supposed to meet, but he wasn't there, recalled and intensified my mourning (my mother was dead, my father was dead, one of my brothers was dead), my loss (I'd lost nature, I'd lost my language, I'd lost the Mother Church, I didn't have a Father Party), my solitude (families today aren't what they used to be, at home I'm always alone, my wife is on her own, my children are on their own, and now he was away).

What was the difference between the days he was there and the days he was away? It was the difference between being able to speak and not being able to speak. When he wasn't there, I sought out people, but it didn't do any good: with others it was impossible to speak. In a certain sense, I discovered that only in analysis does one speak: the analytic situation is the situation in which man speaks. In the world, man speaks to prove himself: there's no one but himself. In analysis, man speaks to belie himself: there is the other. The words that are spoken in analysis cannot be spoken in any other place. On those occasions when a session was cancelled, my nostalgia was heightened, not for my mother, but for her language, our dialect, and it was entirely a nostalgia for words. They had taken away my dialect, and I felt alone. You're never alone so long as you're among people who speak your language. For me, this hasn't happened for many years. My language has disappeared, it no longer exists. The words that I used as a child are no longer understood by anyone, including myself. I'm alone.

A session missed because he had gone away was one thing, and a session missed because I didn't feel like going was another. I didn't want to go when I wanted to punish him. He'd seemed to me indifferent, he'd been a minute late in coming to open the door, and had excused himself by saying he hadn't heard the bell. He was lying. The truth was that he wasn't thinking about me, he'd been reading, or had gone to the toilet. I cocked an ear, trying to hear it flush: nothing, perhaps because the bathroom was in another part of the house. So I wanted to punish him: because he wasn't thinking of me, I wouldn't keep the next appointment. But I didn't stay home: I took the car and drove in the direction of the hills, as though I were going to analysis. Just before reaching his villa, I turned and drove beyond it. There's a road behind it leading to a tavern, high up with a view, almost at the top of a hill. I parked and sat down at a table. From there I could see his house. For a whole hour I sat there watching, while thinking: Have you flushed the toilet? Are you ready for me? Well, I'm not coming. I tried to guess what he was doing: He'll be looking at his watch, he'll have started reading again, he'll be wondering if someone has rung the bell, maybe he'll go and open the door—there's no one. From the top of the hill I stared at his house for the whole session, checking the time myself. When the hour was over, I got back in my car and drove home. So you couldn't say I'd skipped a session: we'd been together, I thinking of him and he of me.

Thus I didn't feel that these sessions had been missed. Missed sessions were only those cancelled by him, when he went away, vanished, without saying either where or why. Then I was alone. I sought out the most crowded movie theater and sat in the middle of the audience, feeling increasingly desperate and alone.

This, I repeat, happened at the beginning of the analysis, in the early years. After four or five years, the sense of abandonment was much diminished, and in the last year it was no longer there. Indeed, I myself found the pace of four sessions a week rather onerous, but I never suggested that we reduce them to three, because in reality they didn't come to more than three: I don't know how it happened, but more and more often either he or I had another engagement, which we preferred to the analysis. At a certain point, I wondered why all these commitments should crop up in his life only now, when in the first years he had almost always been available. And the answer that occurred to me convinced me by its undeniable clarity: he was feeling the same detachment from me as I was from him. This discovery only served to increase our separation. When the summer vacation arrived, and we had necessarily to take a break, we did not set a date for the resumption of our meetings, but agreed that we would get in touch if the need arose.

It didn't arise, and yet the analysis wasn't over. For it to be over, I had first to see him in perspective, to reduce him to a man. So long as he was a magician, something more than a man, I was something less. Analysis is a relationship between weak and powerful, between the weakest and the most powerful.

One day I telephone him and go to see him. He receives me in a sitting room, many books, a fireplace with a lighted fire. There is the smell of wood smoke. We sit in two armchairs in front of the fire. He asks about my work, my wife, my sons.

I ask about him. I know he teaches at the University; he says, yes, he teaches but nobody wants to learn. Every so often he gets up to put more wood on the fire. Finally I can look at him. I look at him. He's a little shorter than I thought, a little thinner, a little older. He makes a few mistakes in our conversation, about my dead mother, about my dream of the heart (he remembers something about it, but has me confused with someone else), even about my profession. They're only details, but they are the very details that have made me understand what I've understood. I have the impression of not having understood it from him, but from myself, through him. And then it comes to me: even in the newest and most revolutionary experiences, you learn only what you already know; and this man with whom I'm speaking, and whom I'm looking at for the first time—so short, so thin, so old—I don't know at all.

Author's note

This is not a diary or a chronicle, with characters drawn from real life, but a novel; in a few instances, real life may have offered me a pretext, but nothing more.